***'If I ask you ab[...]
you be honest?'***

Rachel tensed at Mik[...]
have let that happen,[...]

'Why? You enjoyed it as much as I did.'

She looked at him. 'My reasons are my own. And private. There won't be another such...
occurrence.'

'Oh, won't there?' Mikel growled. And he pulled her to him, his mouth coming down hard on hers.

Rachel's first impulse to thrust him away vanished as heat rose in her to answer the passion in his kiss. Why did it have to be this man, of all men, who evoked such a deep, yearning need?

If only this kiss could last forever. If only she had no past. If only things were different and there was a chance that Mikel...

But Rachel had used up all her 'if onlys' long ago.

Dear Reader,

Welcome to Silhouette Special Edition's six stupendous novels!

We have two fabulous new series kicking off this month: THE STOCKWELLS (*The Tycoon's Instant Daughter*)—a wealthy dynasty where family secrets and unexpected love wreak havoc on the lives of this infamous clan; plus LONE STAR CANYON from Susan Mallery (*The Rancher Next Door*)—where romance and passion are as hot as the burning sun!

Newcomer Tori Carrington joins Special Edition™ this month with an appealing THAT'S MY BABY! story, *Just Eight Months Old…* It's a fine debut. In contrast, *Man With a Mission* is veteran Lindsay McKenna's latest MORGAN'S MERCENARIES novel, which leads us neatly into her longer *Heart of Stone* in July, which will be part of the summer three-in-one volume.

This month you can also go to Venice with Tracy Sinclair and be wooed by an Italian Duke (*Pretend Engagement*) or go NorthWest to Michigan's cooler climes and unravel the secrets of Jane Toombs' *Her Mysterious Houseguest*.

Do enjoy them all and come back to us next month,

The Editors

Her Mysterious Houseguest

JANE TOOMBS

™ SILHOUETTE®

SPECIAL EDITION™

First published in Great Britain 2002
Silhouette Books, Eton House, 18-24 Paradise Road,
Richmond, Surrey TW9 1SR

© Jane Toombs 2001

ISBN 0 373 24391 X

23-0102

Printed and bound in Spain
by Litografia Rosés S.A., Barcelona

JANE TOOMBS

was born in California, raised in the upper peninsula of Michigan, and has moved from New York to Nevada as a result of falling in love with the state and a Nevadan. Jane has five children, two stepchildren and seven grandchildren. Her interests include gardening, reading and knitting.

To Bror and Evy and their black barn

Chapter One

Though not heavy, the cold, persistent rain hadn't let up since he'd crossed the Mackinac Bridge, entering Michigan's Upper Peninsula from the lower one. Mikel Starzov grimaced. Great way to spend his two-month vacation—in the rain. And in the wilderness, besides, since towns had proved to be small and far between. Having been raised in and around New York City, he felt more at home in people places rather than places surrounded by trees.

Not that he regretted the promise he'd made to his colleague, Henderson, on his wedding day. He'd find Steve's bride's missing sister, just as he'd told both Victoria and Steve he would. He might not have expected the search to lead him into such a desolate area, but he meant to live up to his nickname at headquarters, where they called him "Nemesis" because he'd never failed to track down his quarry. This time would be no exception.

The picture he had of Renee Reynaud at thirteen showed a wiry, thin-faced, undeveloped girl with bright red hair, wary amber eyes and freckles. He'd had the computer expert at headquarters make him a composite of what she might look like now, fourteen years later, but the guy had cautioned him about possible variations since puberty tended to bring about impossible-to-predict changes.

If she was still alive, that is. Always a possibility she wasn't. His hunch, though, told him she was still walking the earth. His hunches made him uneasy because he felt following them wasn't professional. And, by damn, a special government agent needed to stay professional at all costs. Still, he and Steve both had survived a couple of times only because he'd paid attention to a hunch.

At the moment he'd better pay attention to where he was. The sign coming up read Ojibway, the village he was looking for. By the time he reached the town, the rain had diminished to a fine mist. Pulling into the first gas station he came to, he filled the tank before asking directions. Buy something and it makes people less suspicious of questions, he thought.

"Aino Saari's?" the man at the inside counter

repeated. "That's easy. Just go down this here street till you come to the bridge on your left. Cross over the river and go a couple miles. Keep looking for a black barn to the left. Old Aino's a joker. Some guy told him no farmer ever painted a barn black and so Aino goes and paints his black as the inside of a cow. Well, you find that barn and there you are."

As he drove on, Mikel realized he'd actually never seen a black barn before, not anywhere he'd been. Saari's would be a first. And, he hoped, the end of his search.

At the same time as the blue pickup ahead of him signaled for a left turn, he spotted the landmark barn and turned into the private driveway behind the pickup, stopping a short distance behind the truck. He watched the driver, an older man, open the door and climb down, coming alert when he saw the man stagger and clutch at the side of the truck. Drunk? Or in trouble? Not waiting to find out, Mikel leaped from his car and hurried to the pickup.

"Are you okay, sir?" he asked when he reached the gray-haired man, whose cap had fallen onto the wet ground.

"Can't make my legs work right," the man gasped.

Mikel slung his arm around the guy's shoulders, close enough now to smell alcohol if liquor was the cause of the problem. When he didn't detect that telltale odor, and the man slumped against him, he decided this was an emergency situation. "Think you can make it to my car?" he asked. "I'll get you to a hospital."

As he half carried the man to the nondescript older car he was driving, a dark-haired woman rushed out of the nearby house, crying, "Aino, what's wrong?"

"Help me get him into my car," Mikel ordered when she came close. "He needs a doctor."

She obeyed without any fuss, and once they eased Aino into the back seat, she got in beside him. "I need directions," Mikel told her as he slid behind the wheel. "You do have a hospital in Ojibway, I hope."

She nodded. "Go right onto the highway, back to town. I'll tell you where to turn when we get there."

While they sped into Ojibway, he heard her murmuring to Aino as she supported his head on her shoulder. When they reached the hospital, Mikel jumped out and hurried into the emergency entrance. Moments later he followed a gurney out to the car and helped the male paramedic extract Aino from the back seat and onto the gurney. Once inside the hospital again, he was relegated to the tiny waiting room while Aino was wheeled off and the young woman steered to a desk to answer questions and sign forms. After a time she joined Mikel in the waiting room.

"They won't let me be with him," she said, her voice breaking.

"Tests to run," he told her, feeling inadequate. His impulse was to put his arms around her for comfort, but now that he had time to notice, she was not only young, but a striking brunette who very likely would misinterpret such a gesture from a stranger.

Blinking back tears, she focused on him. "Thank God you were there to help," she said. "I'm Rachel Hill, Aino's cousin. Oh, I do hope he's going to be all right."

"I hope so, too." Mikel meant every word. The old man might be his only chance to pick up Renee's trail. "My name's Mikel Starzov, by the way."

"You were coming to see Aino?"

He nodded, then added, "Actually I wanted to talk to him about his son Leo." He knew it was always good to toss out a bit of info on the chance of picking up something useful. If she was a relative of Aino's, she must have been acquainted with Leo.

"Leo's been dead for seven years," she said.

"I realize that. Did you know him?"

"Yes." She clenched her hands together. "Do you think if I asked they'd tell me how Aino's doing? I'm so worried about him. "

"I'll go with you."

Mikel managed to catch the attention of a nurse hurrying past.

"Aino Saari?" she said in response to Mikel's inquiry. "Doctor thinks he's suffered a cerebral vascular accident. We'll know more when the tests are done."

"How is he?" Rachel's voice was ragged.

The nurse touched her arm. "He's holding his own. We'll let you see him as soon as possible. I know it's hard to wait." With that she left them.

Watching Rachel's face start to crumple, Mikel decided that now that she knew his name he no longer qualified as a complete stranger and she really did need comfort. He put his arm around her shoulders and led her back to the waiting room. There she leaned against him, crying, and he held her gently, aware she wasn't really aware of him as anything but a fellow human who wanted to help.

Which he was, at least for the moment. He truly wanted to offer what comfort he could to Rachel Hill, the questions could wait. He had to admit, though, he couldn't help being very much aware that she was an attractive young woman who fit perfectly into his arms.

After a few moments, she pulled away. "Eva," she said in a choked voice, fumbling for a tissue.

Mikel came to attention. "Eva?" he repeated, knowing that was the name of Leo's daughter.

Rachel wiped her eyes. "Aino's granddaughter. She's in Finland visiting relatives. I should call her, but…"

"You think it might be better to wait until you know more." It wasn't a question.

"Don't you?"

He could hardly say he'd prefer to have Eva return as soon as possible so he could talk to her about her father and the missing Renee. "Surely they'll let you see Aino soon," he temporized.

She tried to smile at him and her brave effort made his chest tight. This gal was having more of an effect on him than he liked. Cardinal rule—never get involved with anyone, especially a woman, who was connected with a case. He might not be working for the agency in this instance, but that didn't mean the rule didn't apply. The one time he'd violated it had not only nearly cost him his job, but his life as well.

If only Rachel's hair wasn't so black and glossy, her brown eyes so soft and warm. She was more than pretty—gorgeous from head to toe was closer. Strange some guy hadn't snapped her up by now. Come to think of it, maybe one had. "Is there anyone you'd like me to call?" he asked.

Rachel shook her head. "No, with Eva away, there's just Aino and me."

Mikel took that to mean no husband, but he didn't like to admit knowing the fact made him feel better. He was *not* going to get involved.

"Cerebral accident means a stroke, doesn't it?" she said.

"Yes."

Rachel sighed. "He's a good man, he doesn't deserve this."

"No one deserves to be sick."

"You're right. But Aino's special to me. He took me in when I was orphaned. Except for Eva, he's my only relative."

Thinking his questions might distract her from her worry over Aino, Mikel commented, "You said you'd known his son, Leo. Did he live in Ojibway?"

"No, not really. He was a teacher who taught in various Upper Peninsula towns."

"Since he had a daughter I assume he was married."

"His wife died right after he came back to the Upper Peninsula."

"Oh? Then he lived elsewhere before that?"

"He must have. I didn't really know him before he returned here."

Her answers, though brief, came naturally. Mikel was good at detecting lies from truth. He was pretty sure Rachel wasn't lying.

"How about you?" she asked.

"Me?"

"I've told you who my relatives are. It's your turn."

"Grandmother." He hadn't stopped to see Grandma Sonia on his way through New York and felt guilty because he didn't visit as often as he should. She was hale and hearty and perfectly able to care for herself, but he knew she was lonesome since his grandfather died.

"Just one grandmother?"

"That's it."

The nurse they'd talked to appeared in the doorway. "Rachel," she said, "Aino's been transferred to ICU. You can visit him there now, but please keep the visit brief."

"I'll wait here," Mikel said.

Rachel left him there, surprised at her wish that he could come with her. After following the directions she'd been given, she found Aino in the three-bed intensive care unit hooked up to various bags and monitors. He opened his eyes when she stood by his bed.

"Guess this old goat's gonna make it ," he told her.

Rachel bent and kissed his cheek. "You scared me."

"That young man who helped get me here—who was he?"

"His name is Mikel Starzov, that's all I know." Aino didn't need to have her tell him that Mikel was kind and comforting and that she liked him, even though his questions about Leo had made her uneasy.

"The doc says if I hadn't gotten here so quick I might've been in a lot worse shape. He thinks I might come out of this pretty good and we got this Mikel Starzov to thank for that."

She nodded.

"So I want you to invite Mikel to stay at the farm for as long as he has business in the area," Aino continued. "That's the least we can do for a Good Samaritan."

Rachel's instinct was to tell Aino she didn't think that was a good idea, since Mikel's business seemed to involve them, but this was no time to argue with the old man. "Okay," she said.

"Tell Mikel I'll be home in a few days to thank him personally. You take him back to the farm now, no use you hanging around here when the cow will need to be milked. And I don't want you scaring Eva into rushing back from Finland. I'm too ornery to die, Doc said so right out."

As she returned to where Mikel waited, Rachel tried to tell herself he wasn't a threat to them all with his questions. Something about him fascinated her against her will. He was attractive, no doubt about that, with his dark hair and chiseled features, but it was those slightly tilted green eyes that got to her. Hunter's eyes. She took a deep breath. Rachel Hill was no man's prey.

She waited until they were driving away from the hospital to invite him to stay at the farm, saying, "Aino insists. We have a guest cottage so you'll have privacy."

"That's very kind of you," Mikel told her, thinking it was just as well he wouldn't be in the same house with her, the two of them alone, tempting fate.

"Do you mind if I stop to make a phone call on the way?"

"You can use our phone if you like."

"Thanks, but I don't want to trouble you."

He'd spotted an outside phone at the gas station where he'd stopped before and so he pulled in there. Even on vacation he was expected to stay in touch, but private phones could be traced and tapped, so he never made agency calls from anywhere but a pay phone.

He was connected immediately and told his only message was from his grandmother who'd called the Riggs and Robinson screening phone number that led to the agency. She wanted him to get in contact with her immediately.

Before he hung up, he asked his researcher friend, Ed, to check out Rachel Hill, probably born in Michigan twenty odd years ago. Mikel had no reason to mistrust her, but a special agent always made sure.

He'd have to call his grandmother. He really should have taken a detour to see her on the way here—she knew he was on vacation. Taking a deep breath he started to punch in her number, then changed his mind and called his colleague Steve first instead.

"You're where?" Steve asked.

"Ojibway, Michigan, following a lead," Mikel told him. "No real news yet."

"If you're going to be there a few days, I've got some photos of Heidi I want to send you. General delivery?"

"I figure it might take a week or so up here to check things out. Send 'em along."

Mikel smiled as he hung up, Steve thought his adopted baby daughter was the cutest thing on two feet. Which she was, more or less. He called Grandma Sonia then, who, as he'd expected, began to scold him the minute she heard his voice.

"What kind of grandson are you who doesn't come to see his aged grandmother when he's on vacation? For all you know I might be on my last legs."

"As I recall you were wearing shorts when I last saw you," he reminded her, "and your legs looked pretty healthy then."

"A lot can happen in two months, my Mikel. Where have you got yourself to now?"

"I'm in Michigan's Upper Peninsula in a town named Ojibway. Sort of a wilderness area. After all, I'm on vacation."

"Don't try to fool me, young man. You never were one for hunting and fishing or gawking at wildlife. You've got some other reason for being in such a strange place. You're not working, so it can't be that. What is it?"

Mikel sighed inwardly. Try as he might, he'd

never managed to stop Grandma Sonia from asking questions. When he was on agency business, he simply told her he couldn't discuss what he was doing, but it was hard to discourage her natural inquisitiveness otherwise. This might not be agency business, but it was his business and he had no intention of revealing the truth. What could he say to keep her quiet?

A thought struck him, making him smile. She was always trying to marry him off to some girl or other, maybe this would stop her. "I'm seeing a woman," he told her.

"You're interested in some girl up there in the wilderness?"

"Yes."

His smile broadened at the few seconds of silence that followed. Gotcha, he told himself.

"May I ask her name?" Grandma Sonia finally said.

"Rachel Hill." The name was out before he thought to invent a fictitious one. Still, it didn't matter, Ojibway was a long way from White Plains, New York, where his grandmother lived.

"Well, dear, I don't want to keep you," she told him, and hung up before he could promise to come and see her on his way back to his Maryland apartment.

Which wasn't like Sonia, not at all. He'd been preparing himself to field a hundred questions about "his girl" but she hadn't asked a one. Odd. He was still puzzling over it when he got back to the car and found the gas station attendant talking to Rachel through the open window.

"I sure am glad he's gonna be okay," the man said. "Got worried when I heard he was took bad. Wouldn't be the same around here without old Aino." He waved at Mikel and walked back to the building.

"News travels fast in these parts," Mikel commented as he started the car.

"You can't keep a secret in a small town," Rachel agreed.

If that was true, then sooner or later someone in the vicinity was bound to know the answers to Mikel's questions.

"I have some pasties ready to bake," she added. "I was about to turn the oven on when I looked out and saw you there in the driveway holding on to Aino. You're welcome to have supper with me."

"Pasties?"

"Cornish meat pies. Except not quite, because we Finns put carrots in them, something a true Cornishman would never, ever do. "

"Since I'm not Cornish, I won't quibble. Thanks for the invitation."

"I'll be putting the food on the table in about an hour and a half," she told him.

Once they arrived at the farm, she gave him the key to the small cottage and he settled himself in, finding the place a bit chilly even though the rain had stopped completely. He decided to light a fire in the fireplace so it'd be warm when he came back to the cottage after supper, as Rachel had called the meal.

Once he got a blaze going he sank into an old armchair, propped his feet on the matching stool and relaxed, thinking it'd been a long time since he'd sat in front of a real fire. Rarely did any agency investigation lead him to such a snug and cozy spot. But this time he was on his own. Was Renee to be found here in Ojibway?

He'd come to the Upper Peninsula, following the only lead he'd been able to uncover. Victoria hadn't been able to tell him much. She'd been eleven when her sister disappeared and vaguely remembered that Renee once had a crush on a teacher of hers—a man named Leo Saari. Then she'd given Mikel her mother's address in Florida.

He'd flown down to see Mrs. Reynaud, who was living in a retirement village and had unearthed a few more facts. She'd told him Renee had sometimes baby-sat Leo Saari's daughter, even though Mr. Reynaud had forbidden his daughters to go anywhere other than school without their mother. Baby-sitting was therefore out of the question unless Renee's mother had covered up for her daughter, which she admitted having done.

Rusty Reynaud had been a mean alcoholic, an abusive type, according to both Victoria and her mother. They were all terrified of him, especially when he got out his old Colt .45 with the elk embossed on the grip and aimed it at them, threatening to shoot. If Renee had run off, it was no wonder. But it was strange the Colt had disappeared at the same time she did.

Mikel stared into the dancing flames as if they held the answer to what had happened to that thirteen-year-old girl. Her old man hadn't killed her, because a month after Renee vanished, the mother got a phone call from her, though she'd never told this to Victoria. Before Renee could say much of anything, the father had grabbed the phone, cursed her and demanded she return his gun, threatening he'd find her no matter where she hid. Understandably, the girl had hung up and the family never heard from her again.

Soon after that, the mother packed up and moved with Victoria to another state. Two years later she heard her husband had died. A relief to everyone, Mikel was sure.

Mikel had then checked with the police in what had been the Reynauds' New Jersey hometown. He learned that the same night Renee had disappeared there had been a shooting in town. A drug dealer had been killed by a bullet from a Colt .45, which was never found. Although Mikel had learned that Rusty Reynaud had been chummy with the dead man, there was no concrete evidence to connect him to the shooting, especially since another thug had left town just about the same time.

With that lead a dead end, Mikel had checked the school Renee had attended. The principal had told him that Leo Saari had resigned the month before Renee had disappeared to care for his sick wife. Saari had given Ojibway, Michigan, as his forwarding address. Although the principal had no idea when Saari had left town, he thought it seemed logical it would've been not too long after he resigned.

This brought Mikel's attention back to what Renee's mother had confessed to him. She'd never told her husband where their daughter was headed that fateful afternoon for fear of his rage. Renee had gone off by herself to baby-sit the Saari child, making Mikel wonder if she'd ever arrived. No one had asked at the time, because Renee's mother had been afraid to speak up.

But it meant Saari had still been in town on that day. Though it didn't pinpoint the exact date of his departure, the coincidence had made Mikel suspicious. So, fourteen years later, he was here in Ojibway, where Leo Saari moved to, trying to trace a possible connection between Saari and the missing girl. Though Leo was no longer alive now, surely if he'd brought a red-haired girl with him all those years ago some people around here would remember.

Certainly his father would. Unfortunately, at the moment, Aino was in no condition to be asked questions. But Rachel Hill was available. For questioning, that is. Not for anything else, Mikel cautioned himself, no matter how well she'd fit into his arms.

The chair was so comfortable and the fire so pleasantly warm that he hated to move. All the cottage lacked was someone for him to share this interlude with.

A female someone. In his mind's eye he pictured a leggy brunette whose soft brown eyes promised a sweetness he didn't see too much of in the women he knew. She wasn't all that far away, either.

What harm was there in imagining her here with him? In reality, far from practical, but no problem at all in a daydream. Rachel had worn no makeup, her pink lips, free of gloss, had looked eminently kissable. He recalled her scent, something faintly flowery but elusive, an enticing fragrance that was on the tip of his memory.

If she were here in this chair with him, he might be able to place that elusive scent. And taste those enticing pink lips. Among other things that he'd best not dwell on or he'd be in no shape to go to the farmhouse for supper.

Chapter Two

Once the pasties were in the oven, Rachel went out, collected the cow from the field and led her to her stall in the barn. There, she pulled on her coveralls and sat down to milk her. When she finished she placed the milk in the cooler, shed the coveralls and returned to the house where she washed up.

Eyeing her jeans and T-shirt, she decided to change to a pants outfit more intermediate—not jeans, but not dressy, either. She had no need, or reason, to dress up for Mikel, though she did need a few dabs of makeup. But when she found herself fussing with her hair, she made a face at herself in the mirror, put the brush away and marched out of her bedroom.

In the big old farm kitchen, she set the pine table with everyday dishes and silverware, not wanting Mikel to get the idea the meal was a special event for his sake. It was merely the supper she'd planned for herself and Aino, not a good-china-and-silver-dining-room dinner.

As she finished making the salad the oven chime went off, telling her the meal was cooked. After setting the salad bowl on the table she grabbed a hot pad and removed the sheet of pasties from the oven. She glanced at the phone, which hadn't rung since the doctor had called to tell her Aino's prognosis looked promising. He'd said he believed the immediate treatment he'd been able to give Aino had prevented a more serious stroke. And, yes, she'd be notified if there was any change for the worse—which he didn't expect.

Of course she was still worried about Aino, but that wasn't why she was as jittery as a teenager on a first date. Which this certainly wasn't. Inviting Mikel to supper was a mere courtesy and bore no possible resemblance to a date. Well, maybe a little something other than courtesy. She needed to discover exactly why he'd come here to locate a man who'd been dead for seven years, and a good way to find out was to be casually friendly over food.

Transferring five of the pasties to a plate, she set it on the table next to the salad, then plucked the ketchup bottle from the refrigerator and added that. Aino always slathered ketchup on his pasty. Never mind what Martha Stewart might say, the bottle on the table made it all the more casual.

Even though she'd been expecting it, when she heard the tap at the kitchen door she started and had to clear her throat before calling, "Come in."

"Something smells mouthwatering good in here," Mikel said as he entered.

She gestured toward the table, wordlessly inviting him to be seated.

"Anything I can do?" he asked, hovering instead of sitting, looking at her with those green hunter's eyes.

"Just tell me if you want coffee with supper or afterward."

"After, please."

When she started toward the table, he held her chair out for her and pushed it in once she sat down, just as though they were in some fancy restaurant. She appreciated his gesture, even though it made her more nervous for some reason.

"I hope you like the pasties," she said.

"My grandmother taught me early to approach any new dish with a confident heart, as she put it, meaning that I should expect it to be delicious."

As he spoke, he slid a pasty onto his plate. Picking up his fork, he used it to break through the crust and lifted out a portion filled with vegetables and meat. As he chewed he raised his left hand and formed an approving circle with his thumb and forefinger.

She gestured toward the ketchup bottle. "Aino likes to pour ketchup over his pasty."

Mikel shook his head. "I don't fool with perfection."

Though pleased, she told herself she wasn't getting any further with her plan to find out why he'd come here. What did he want to know about Leo?

He looked out a window, saying, "Even on a cloudy day you have long summer twilights here."

Rather than wasting time commenting on northern summer evenings, she tried to find an opening that wasn't too obvious. "Have you ever visited the U.P. before?" she asked finally.

"No. Do you always get these cold rains in August?"

"Some years. It'll warm up." How could she ease him off small talk?

"Did you hear how your grandfather is doing?" he said after a short silence.

"The doctor is optimistic."

"So that means you won't have to call his granddaughter in Finland right away. How long before she comes back to the States?"

She had her opening. "Why do you ask?"

"Because I'd like to talk to her."

"About what?"

He raised an eyebrow. "How about a fair exchange here? You haven't yet answered my question."

It wouldn't do any harm to tell him, she decided.

"Eva will be flying back to New York City the end of next week, but, before driving home, I think she plans to stay awhile with the upstate friend she left her car with."

"So my questions will have to wait. "

"I still don't understand why you want to talk to her."

Evaluating her comments, Mikel decided she didn't sound particularly defensive, just curious. Those soft brown eyes hadn't blinked too many or too few times and she met his gaze normally. Liars tended to either look away or keep fixed on the person they spoke to.

"I realize you must want to know what I'm doing here in Ojibway," he said. "Fourteen years ago a girl disappeared from her home back East. Her name is Renee Reynaud and she was thirteen at the time. I'm searching for her."

Though she didn't respond immediately, he noted that Rachel's expression of polite curiosity didn't change, reassuring him of her honesty. "I don't understand why you're searching here," she said.

"Leo Saari was one of Rachel's teachers and she sometimes baby-sat his daughter. He left that same New Jersey community about the time Rachel disappeared and I learned that he'd come to Ojibway. I'm checking out every possible connection. I was hoping Aino would be able to tell me if Leo had a red-haired little girl with him when he arrived here, but I don't want to pester him with questions until he's recovered. Eva may be able to remember a few things about Renee that might help me.''

''Eva was only eight when her father returned home. She might be rather hazy about an early baby-sitter.''

''You're protective of Eva.''

Rachel gave him a level look. ''Maybe so. I tend to feel like her older sister. But as for asking if Leo arrived here with a red-haired girl, I can answer that. Like everyone else around Ojibway, I know the only people with him were his wife and daughter Eva. Poor Mrs. Saari died not long after they got here.''

He had no reason not to believe her, though he'd ask around to be sure. ''I'd still like to talk to Eva, even if I have to wait until she gets back. I don't expect you to put me up for what may be several weeks so I'll look for—''

Rachel cut him off. ''Aino will be upset if you don't stay at the farm. It's his way of repaying you for your timely help.''

Mikel didn't argue. It suited him to be right where he was, handy to those who might offer some clues to what had happened to Renee. Not to mention seeing more of Rachel, whether that was wise or not.

''Is that what you do for a living?'' Rachel asked ''Search for missing persons?''

''It's part of my job, yes.'' Which it was. She

didn't need to know those he searched for were usually criminals. "What do you do?"

"I teach English and drama at the Ojibway High School." She rose and began clearing the table, declining his help.

When she served the coffee, she also brought a plate of chocolate cookies with chocolate frosting. "My compliments to the chef," he said after the first bite.

She smiled, the first genuine smile she'd given him. "Those are Aunt Sally's Cocoa Drops, but don't ask who Aunt Sally is. No one has a clue."

He'd noticed there was no automatic dishwasher so he said, "I do know my way around a kitchen, thanks to Grandma Sonia, who insisted chores were a unisex thing, not divided into male and female duties. I'll help you with the dishes as thanks for a great meal."

"Did your grandmother live with you?" she asked.

He shook his head. "Like you, I was orphaned young. My grandparents raised me."

"Then you can understand how much Aino means to me. I'd do anything for him."

She sounded so fierce he smiled inwardly. Rachel was protective of her own, a trait he could understand.

After they finished the coffee and cookies, he pitched in to help clean up and she didn't argue. He found he enjoyed working alongside her, leading him to wonder what it'd be like if he actually had a permanent home and someone to share it with. *Back off from that thought, Starzov,* he warned himself. *Even if that's what you wanted, and it's decidedly not, this gal is off-limits.*

"I'm going to the hospital to visit Aino," she told him when they finished.

Despite knowing better, he wanted to prolong that feeling of companionship. "I'll drive you, if you like," he offered.

"Nice of you, but no thanks."

"Then I presume it's good-night." He headed for the back door as he spoke.

She followed, saying, "If you like you can have breakfast here."

He paused, turning to look at her. "I don't want to take advantage of your hospitality. Just give me the name of a good place to eat in town."

"Sylvia's. It's near the bridge. Well, good night, then."

He hesitated, fighting the crazy impulse to kiss her in parting, then left the house. As he sauntered toward the cottage he saw the clouds had parted, giving him a view of the darkening evening sky where a single star shone. He glanced at the black barn and the other outbuildings with the feeling something was missing. A dog, that's what. Most farms he'd been to in line with his job had dogs that threatened intruders. The Saaris didn't. Yet here he was, the intruder.

Smoke rose from the cottage chimney, a welcome reminder it would be warm inside. In the morning, he'd have breakfast at Sylvia's where, if he was lucky, he could begin the process of what his boss called "chatting up the townsfolk," usually a good source of information if done casually enough. Most people loved to talk.

Once inside, he checked the place where he'd cached his gun to be sure it was there. This wasn't the kind of case where he anticipated needing a gun, but he'd learned never to take chances. Easing down into the armchair, he stared into the fire, reduced now to half-burned logs licked by tiny flames. Knowing exactly where his gun was reassured him even though nothing threatened him here. Nothing but a long-legged gal with dark hair, warm brown eyes and a body that fit against his just right. He'd avoided brunettes since Yolanda—that treacherous woman from his past—but Rachel was so very different from the women he usually met—no sharp edges, no hidden agendas.

Careful about snap judgments, man, he warned himself. You don't really know her, just like you didn't really know Yolanda and your carelessness there damn near killed you.

But Yolanda was in the past. Behind him for good. There was no danger in admiring Rachel. He closed his eyes, imagining she'd come back to the cottage with him. All he had to do was pull her down onto his lap and....

Enough! Damned if he wasn't fantasizing like a fool high school kid. One with a crush on his English teacher. Which probably every male student in her class did have. Relax. Savor the comfort you're enjoying here and now. Most cases don't set you up in such cozy surroundings. Take it easy.

He tried one of the breathing techniques he'd been taught, but Yolanda's image returned to plague him.

He'd trusted her, been completely taken in by her act. No excuse. A special agent knew better. He'd been lucky not to get booted out of the agency for blowing the case. Would have been if Steve hadn't stood up for him.

Two nights ago he'd had that blasted recurring nightmare about what had happened. He didn't believe in dreams as warnings, but, as he eased into bed, he told himself maybe he ought to begin doing just that here and now.

Back from the hospital, Rachel got ready for bed, wondering why on earth Aino had insisted she bring Mikel to see him tomorrow. She'd reminded him only relatives could visit the ICU, but he'd insisted he'd be moving to a regular room first thing in the morning so there'd be no problem. Since this was no time to burden him with any kind of worry, she hadn't said anything about why Mikel was in Ojibway.

Mikel had told her he didn't want to question

Aino while he was recuperating, but could she trust him to keep his word? Her experience with men other than Leo and Aino had been that they always looked out for themselves first. Why should Mikel be different? And why did she want him to be? What was there about him that appealed to her against her will?

Not his looks, great as those were. She felt drawn to him in a way she didn't understand. Perhaps it was because they'd shared that worrisome time in the hospital waiting room while Aino was being examined. Whatever it was, she'd do well to forget about sharing anything else with Mikel. He was here only to find a missing girl, and when he discovered she was nowhere around, he'd leave.

Strange, though, she'd had the oddest feeling he was going to kiss her there at the back door when they said good-night. Naturally, she wouldn't have let him. Would she? Shaking her head, she glanced from her bedroom window, seeing the light still on in the cottage. With a sigh, she slid under the covers, knowing sleep would take its time coming....

The path ahead wound through the trees where deep shadows lay in wait. If there'd been any other way to get where she needed to go, she would have chosen it. If only she weren't alone, but she knew she had to be, part of the test was being alone. This time she wouldn't fail, this time she'd reach her goal. Still, she hesitated before taking her first step into that dark woods. She hated not being able to see if any danger lurked in the shadows.

Since there was no choice but to go on, she took a fortifying breath and plunged into the darkness, trying not to panic, not to run lest she lose the trail. Her arms prickled with goose bumps as she felt unknown menace on either side. A noise from behind made her spine crawl with dread. If she turned to look, what might she see? Despite herself, she began to hurry faster and faster, her head turning from side to side as she watched the shadows.

Because she wasn't paying attention to where she stepped, she tripped and started to fall. But something caught her, held her up. Rescuing her? As she stared at the dark figure who held her, a moonbeam slipped through the trees to light up his eyes. Green hunter's eyes. She tried to scream but no sound emerged, tried to break free but couldn't move. He'd trapped her....

Rachel sat bolt upright in bed, heart pounding. For a moment or two the dream clung to her so that she couldn't orient herself, then reason returned. She was safe in her own room, in her own bed. Safe and sound.

But for how long?

Taking a deep breath, she brushed aside that thought. Rachel Hill could control her own destiny. Hadn't she been doing just that for more years than she cared to count? She was secure in herself, which she ought to be, considering all the practice she'd had.

Mikel Starzov might be the most attractive and sexy man she'd ever met, but he was an outsider and would be leaving in a week or so. The threat he posed would be gone, and they'd all be safe again.

Why, then, did she remember so clearly how he'd comforted her in the ER waiting room, holding her against him, letting her draw strength from the contact. If she'd felt a tad more than comfort, that was her business. Certainly he'd never find out. It was as simple as that.

But in her heart she knew she wasn't telling herself the truth. She'd never before encountered a man like Mikel and she was already certain he wouldn't be easily forgotten.

Chapter Three

The next morning, Mikel found quite a crowd having breakfast in Sylvia's and no empty tables or booths. A waving hand caught his attention and he recognized the gas station attendant.

"Got an extra chair right here," the man said. "You're welcome to it."

"Thanks." Mikel seated himself, giving his name.

"Hi, Mikel, I'm Bob and this here's my buddy, Louie." Introductions over, Bob asked, "How's old Aino doing?"

"Pretty good, the last I heard."

"Seen you with Ráchel yesterday—you a relative?"

Mikel shook his head. Choosing his words carefully—questions didn't work as well as offering small snippets of information—he said, "I knew Aino's son, Leo. I wasn't around when Leo died, so this is my first chance to visit Aino."

Louie grimaced. "That Leo was some magnet for bad luck. First his wife dies, then her folks drop one after the other. Aino's wife was next to go. Almost like the guy was cursed or something."

After the waitress came over and took his order, Mikel brought the subject back to where he wanted by saying, "Leo died pretty young."

"Got himself killed, that's what he did," Bob said. "Most often you don't buy the farm when your car hits a deer, but like Louie told you, Leo was unlucky, poor guy."

The waitress, bringing Mikel's coffee, heard the last and said, "The one I felt sorry for was Aino's cousin. Rachel had to take care of Eva after that. No one else left 'cept Aino. That's why he took the two of them in after Leo got killed."

"Heck, Dottie, Rachel must've been somewhere in her twenties when Leo died and she'd been taking care of Eva all along."

"Yeah, but it was different when Eva's dad was alive." Dottie threw the words over her shoulder as, coffeepot in hand, she went to serve another table.

"You never get the last word with Dottie," Louie confided.

"I lost touch with Leo when he moved back to the U.P.," Mikel said. "Rachel told me he taught in several different towns up here."

Bob nodded. "Never seemed satisfied in one place. He dragged them two kids around with him—Rachel wasn't much more than a kid herself then, but she was old enough to look after Eva and that's what he needed."

"Just as well," Louie put in. "Aino was too old to be raising young girls without a woman to help out. It's different now the girls are old enough—they take care of him."

Bob, through with his meal, pushed back his chair and rose. "Time to get going. See you around, Mikel." Louie nodded to Mikel and followed Bob from the café.

Dottie brought the eggs and bacon Mikel had ordered, asking if he wanted more coffee. At his nod, she brought the pot. "You don't want to believe everything them two characters tell you," she said.

Looking at the fortyish woman, he noticed her eyes were an unusual aquamarine color. "I didn't realize Rachel had lived with Leo and his daughter," he said.

"Oh, sure. It was pure luck for him that the Saaris took Rachel in after her folks died downstate. There she was, waiting, so to speak. Otherwise he'd've had to hire someone, and I want to tell you, teachers don't make all that much money. My sister's one and I know."

As he ate breakfast, Mikel wondered why Rachel hadn't mentioned the fact she'd lived with Leo, raising his daughter until he died. On the other hand, why should she when she didn't know him? He hadn't asked her, so he shouldn't make something from what was probably nothing. It did explain why she felt so protective of Eva.

He reminded himself she was an orphan, as he was. Aino had taken her in the way his grandparents had Mikel.

After he finished eating, he decided to drop by the hospital to ask how Aino was doing. When he did, the receptionist told him Aino had been moved to a private room. "Are you Mikel Starzov?" she inquired. When he nodded, she added, "Aino's been asking to see you. He's in room 224. Just down the hall and to the right."

Mikel found Rachel with the old man and greeted them both, trying to ignore the unexpected leap of his heart when he saw her.

"Good to see you, young man," Aino told him. "Come closer so I can shake your hand. Doc says if you hadn't gotten me here so quick I might not be shaking hands with anyone for a while, if ever."

"Yes, and he scolded you for not taking the medicine he gave you for your high blood pressure," Rachel added.

Aino waved that away. "I know, I know." Finished with the handshake, he gave Mikel an assessing once-over, finally nodding. "You'll do. Call me Aino. Rachel tells me she's got you set up in the cottage. That's good. ''

"Very comfortable quarters.''

"You did me a favor getting me here, now I got another to ask. Thought I'd be out of here by tomorrow, but Doc says not yet. He says I had a ministroke and that's why my left arm's so weak. The leg's not as bad. So I got to have therapy for it and he's still got some tests to run. I swear they're going to drain off all my blood before I get out of here. The point is, I want you to stay at the farm at least till I come home. We lost old Fitzgerald last month and I don't like Rachel out there all alone.''

"Fitzgerald?'' Mikel repeated.

"My rabbit hound. Died of old age. Always name my dogs after someone I know.''

"Someone he knows and doesn't like,'' Rachel explained. She focused on Aino. "I wish you'd listen to me. I've told you over and over I'm perfectly all right out there by myself.''

"Don't want me to get set back by worry, do you?''

She rolled her eyes.

"I'll be happy to stay in the cottage,'' Mikel said.

"Good boy. One more thing. I was supposed to give Rachel's Girl Scout troop a talk about Johnny Appleseed and why all of us should plant trees whenever we can. Was going to demonstrate how and where to plant a tree. Got a bunch of apple seedlings in cans on the back porch. I'm thinking you could take over for me.''

Mikel had never planted a tree in his life. He hadn't ever considered planting one, either. Before he could answer, evidently Aino saw the doubt in his eyes.

''Nothing to it, boy. I'd let Rachel do it, but she's always teaching them things. They'll take it more serious-like if you doing the talking and the showing. Right, girl?''

Rachel shrugged.

''You know it's true, that's why you got me to do it,'' Aino said. ''So Mikel will be my substitute.'' He winked at Rachel. ''Teachers know all about substitutes.''

''I'll do what I can,'' Mikel promised, ''but I'm not Johnny Appleseed.''

''None of us are, boy. Just as well, what'd we do with all those apples? Rachel knows how trees are planted, she can tell you whatever you don't know.''

A hospital worker arrived with a wheelchair to take Aino for therapy, so Rachel and Mikel left. Pausing by her car in the parking lot, he said, ''How about letting me take you to dinner tonight? It's my turn.''

''Do you like fish?''

Strange thing about women, they almost never answered precisely what was asked. ''All kinds,'' he told her.

"Good. Because this, like every Friday, is fish-fry night in the U.P."

"In that case, you choose where."

"Metrovich's is usually good But we'll need to get there early before they run out of perch—it's their specialty. Say five-thirty."

He nodded. "I'll drive. About this Johnny Appleseed deal. I've never talked to a Girl Scout troop before."

She smiled, rather smugly, he thought. "Don't worry, the girls will hang on your every word."

He eyed her dubiously.

"As for the tree planting," she added, "I'll give you a quick run-through ahead of time. You can read up on the original Johnny later tonight."

"My bedtime story? Okay, but I've never been one for planting things."

"Tell them that. They'll listen to you, watch you plant a seedling and be impressed that this cool guy is interested in trees. You'll make a great role model."

His eyebrows rose. "I've been called lot of things, but never that."

"Consider it from their point of view. They may like me, but I'm just their predictable Scout leader who's always going on about what's important. You're a—well, let's say a noticeable man from somewhere other than the U.P., as they can tell by the way you talk."

"A 'noticeable' man? Because I'm a stranger?"

She eyed him levelly. "You're the kind of man girls notice. Especially since you always wear black—or at least you have since I've known you."

He blinked. Wearing black had gotten to be a habit without him noticing. Bad for a special agent to do something that identifiable. He'd get some other clothes when he left here. Smiling at her, he asked, "So you think girls notice me? How about a particular young woman?"

"Under the circumstances surrounding your arrival, I could hardly help it." Her words were cool enough, but he noted her flush with interest. So the attraction wasn't only on his side.

Rachel, unhappily aware of her blush, tried to ignore it. "I assume," she continued, "since you're searching for a missing girl, you're some kind of private investigator, which will also fascinate the girls."

Though he didn't say yes, he didn't deny it, so Rachel decided she'd hit the nail on the head. She couldn't help wondering who'd hired him to hunt Renee Reynaud down. And why, after fourteen years? If she was careful and clever, maybe she could find out.

"I have errands, so I'll see you back at the house later," she said. He promptly opened the driver's door for her and she slid in, saying, "Bye."

While doing her grocery shopping, she kept reviewing her clothes, trying to decide what to wear tonight. There was no decent place to shop for clothes in town and she certainly wasn't going to drive forty miles just to buy an outfit to go to Metrovich's, which was a casual kind of place.

Still, it mattered to her how she'd look. Because of Mikel. Surely the man knew he appealed to women. He had to be the sexiest man she'd ever met. And, just possibly, the most dangerous. But she'd rather not dwell on that.

She pictured him planting seedlings with the girls in her troop and snickered. He was the least likely Johnny Appleseed in the world. Aino tended to outlandish notions, such as the black barn, but using Mikel as a substitute was one she could appreciate.

Arriving back at the farm, Rachel noted Mikel's car was not parked by the cottage. She was carrying in the last grocery bag when she noticed him pull into the driveway and watched surreptitiously from the kitchen window as he lifted a small box from his car and took it with him into the cottage along with a plastic grocery bag. Shrugging, she turned away. There was no reason and probably nothing to learn from spying on him. If she didn't label it spying, then she'd have to admit she liked to look at him.

He moved like an athlete, no wasted motion, graceful and purposeful as a wolf. Since wolves had been reintroduced to the U.P., she'd spotted one or two and been impressed. Predators. Beautiful predators. Like Mikel.

A predator she was having dinner with tonight.

What should she wear? Everything she owned could be classified as respectable. For most of her life she hadn't wanted to attract undue attention. She sort of camouflaged herself—like prey. Which she was not!

Upstairs, she riffled through the hangers in her closet and sighed. Nothing. Heaven knows anything at all would be okay for Metrovich's, but she was determined to look different tonight in some way or other. Struck by a thought, she hurried into Eva's bedroom. Eva was a tad more buxom than she, top and bottom, but just maybe there was something Eva hadn't packed when she left for Finland.

A half hour passed before she triumphantly carried out a pair of sleek black leather pants and a see-through black silk blouse. The pants fit her perfectly, not too tight, but revealing enough to suit her present mood. As for the ruffled blouse, once she dug up the only black bra she owned, the blouse would complement the leather pants to perfection. It amused her to think that, if Mikel dressed as usual, they'd both be wearing black. She enjoyed the idea she'd be making a statement.

Smiling, she tossed the clothes onto her bed and went downstairs to fix lunch before she began the afternoon chores. After eating, she located the book that had the story of Johnny Appleseed in it and also a pamphlet on tree planting and left them on a table by the door.

Later, Mikel found her out in back where she was

picking apples to take to Aino—Transparents, which were his favorites. "Here," she said, tossing one to Mikel.

"I take it green, in this case, is ripe," he said.

"My, so suspicious."

"Why not? Since Eve persuaded Adam to eat an apple, things have never been the same."

"But this isn't Paradise."

She didn't realize how relaxing the quiet and peace of the farm were, Mikel thought. Hell, even he was surprised at how relaxed he felt. "Close enough," he told her, "but I'll chance the apple." He took a bite.

"What's the verdict?"

"Hmm, a hint of tartness within the sweet, summery flavor. A good year."

She laughed. "Hey, it's only an apple, not fine wine."

"But this is a special one." Like you, he wanted to add, but had enough sense not to. With the sunshine gleaming on her dark wavy hair as she smiled up at him, her brown eyes still crinkled with laughter, she was the most beautiful woman he'd ever seen. Flaws tended to show up in sunlight, but if Rachel had any, they weren't visible.

"Metrovich's is pretty casual, in case you wondered," she said.

"Figures. Most of what I've seen of the U.P. seems to be. It's a different world up here."

"That's why a lot of us never leave."

"How about you?"

A flicker of some emotion couldn't identify crossed her face and disappeared. "Sometimes I think it must be the only safe place left in the world," she said so softly he hardly heard her words.

Seeing an opening, he said, "It must have been difficult raising Eva while you were still a child yourself."

She turned away from him to pick another apple from the tree, speaking with her back to him. "I was glad to have a way to give in return for what others had given me. Besides, Eva was a pretty good kid, as kids go." She dropped the apple into a sack with others. "That's seven apples, more than enough for Aino. He's complaining about hospital food so I plan to take these in to him before we go to dinner."

It was obvious she didn't want to discuss the subject. He didn't have a clue why. After all, it didn't matter. Rachel raising Leo's daughter had no bearing on what he'd come here to do—find Renee Reynaud. Eva, herself, might prove to be of more help than Rachel, since she'd actually known Renee.

"I'm looking forward to meeting Eva," he said.

Ignoring his comment, Rachel said, "Shall I show you the apple tree seedlings on the back porch?"

Reminded of his upcoming duties as a planter, he nodded, hoping the guys at headquarters would never hear he'd spent part of his vacation playing at being Johnny Appleseed.

He surveyed the motley containers the tiny trees were growing in—everything from coffee cans to cardboard cartons and said, "Looks as though Aino recycles everything."

"Farmers always have, didn't you know?"

"If these seedlings get put in a hole in the ground, will they all grow?" he asked.

"It's a little more complicated than that."

He sighed. "I figured it would be. I know zip about plants—Grandma Sonia handled the ones growing in the house. I remember her talking to the droopy fern in the entry, coaxing it to do better."

"Did it?"

"Come to think of it, I don't know what happened to that fern. It never did show up after my grandparents moved to the condo in White Plains."

"You didn't have an outside plot to grow things in when you were a kid?"

"I remember a big tree in back of the apartment complex in the city that shed leaves all over the place in the fall. With that tiny yard, it didn't leave room for much else."

"Let me get what you need to read for your demonstration tomorrow. You can give them a quick run-through while I go visit Aino and, when I get back, we'll discuss how-to."

He grinned. "How-to?"

She shook her head at him and entered the house.

His smile faded as he gazed at the fragile-looking seedlings in the pots. How had he let himself get talked into this, anyway?

Rachel returned briefly to hand him a book and a pamphlet, then disappeared. Easing onto the bench swing suspended by hooks from the porch overhang, he sat with the books in his lap, thinking about Rachel instead of trying to read any of the material she'd given him.

She couldn't be less like Yolanda, he told himself. She was neither self-seeking nor dishonest. No denying she *was* connected with this case, though. His case, not an agency one, yet still business, not pleasure. He'd vowed never to be fooled again by a woman, especially while working. But it was getting more and more difficult to resist his attraction to Rachel. Damn it, he wanted to hold her, to feel her respond to him, to make love to her.

What could possibly be the harm in a brief affair? Because it would be. Other than the fact he wouldn't be here long, he took care to make sure not to get involved in any long-term entanglement. No strings.

He had no inclination to change his lifestyle— why should he? So far, it'd been working out just fine. The women he met were out for a good time— they had no more desire to tie themselves down than he did. No one got hurt and no regrets.

''Wait'll you fall in love, old buddy,'' Steve had

once said to him. "I hope I'm around when it happens, so I can be the first to say I told you so."

"In love? Whatever that means, it has nothing to do with me so you may just be waiting around forever." That had been his answer then and was now.

Love wasn't on his agenda. How could you fall in love with any woman, when there were no honest ones?

Chapter Four

Hearing Mikel whistle at her as she sauntered toward his car on the way to dinner, Rachel smiled to herself, thinking the whistle made it worth the trouble she'd taken.

"Whoa," he said as he opened the passenger door for her. "English teachers didn't wear black leather pants when I was in school."

"I'm not a teacher at the moment."

"Care to tell me what you are?"

"Definitely not prey."

He blinked, but she didn't explain. Evidently deciding to leave well enough alone, he shut her door, went around to the driver's side and slid behind the wheel, saying, "Which way?"

"Turn to the left. Metrovich's is on the way to the Porcupines."

"Porcupines?"

"Mountains. One of our biggest tourist attractions. I'll drive up there with you sometime, if you like. There's an old mine and terrific views. Aino claims the road the state put in when they made the Porcupine Mountains a park took all the fun out of climbing up to the escarpment. That was way before my time, though."

"I'd like to see the park. How's the skiing up there?"

"We get a lot of snow, so it's some of the best. Eva's really good."

"You?"

She shrugged. "Fair. I really enjoy it, though. How about you?"

"I do okay."

She just bet he did. It was difficult to imagine Mikel not excelling at anything physical.

"Care to explain that prey comment?" he asked.

Did this man never leave anything alone? Affecting a casual tone, she said, "Oh, nothing much. Except I suddenly decided my wardrobe was pretty drab—making me look like a little brown bird blending into the underbrush. These are actually Eva's clothes."

"Believe me, no man could overlook you even if you wore sackcloth and ashes."

He spoke with such conviction, she was tempted

to believe him. She certainly wanted to believe he found her attractive.

"And in that outfit—" he glanced at her "—I can see I'll be fending off the locals all night." Grinning, he added, "I trust duels have been outlawed in the U.P. 'cause I did fail to pack my dueling pistols."

To his surprise, she shuddered. "I hate guns!"

Some women did, of course, but her reaction seemed unusually strong, since she must have known he was joking. Searching for a change of topic, he said, "I bought a coffeemaker today for the cottage."

She stared at him. "You didn't have to do that. We always keep a pot on up at the house."

"I'm sure, but I plan to invite you into the cottage for coffee after dinner tonight and so I needed the proper equipment."

"You really think I might accept?" Her tone had lightened.

"Hope springs eternal. I've also laid a fire, ready to be lit against the coolth of the evening."

She smiled. "Coolth?"

"That's U.P. weather," he told her. "Everything's different in this part of the country." Or seemed to be, anyway, since he'd met Rachel.

When they reached Metrovich's—and none too soon by the looks of the crowded parking lot—he anticipated with relish everyone's reaction when they entered. If, as she said, she didn't usually wear black leather pants and see-through blouses, there was bound to be one.

He wasn't disappointed. As they walked past the bar on the way to the dining area, every male in the place did a double take. Mikel felt a purely masculine rush from being Rachel's escort.

At the table, the waitress took a long look at Rachel. "Holy smoke!" she exclaimed. "What on earth did you do to yourself?"

"Borrowed Eva's clothes," Rachel said. "That's all, Kelly."

Kelly slanted a glance at Mikel. "Okay, but where'd you borrow him and have they got any more?"

"He's one of a kind," Rachel told her.

"Figures. I never get there first. You both gonna have the perch tonight?"

While they waited for their order, Mikel checked out the place, a habit he couldn't break, even when he wasn't on an agency case. He'd also chosen the only table left where his back could be to the wall. Rustic, without any attempt to be cutesy as well, Metrovich's looked like what it was, an older, out-of-the-way eating place in the Michigan woods. A place where the local folk gathered.

"What do you think?" Rachel asked. "Acceptable to a New Yorker?"

"I always wait until the food comes to comment. That's what counts."

"In that case, you'll give Metrovich's five stars."

At the moment, anyplace he could be with her would suit him, even a moderately noisy, definitely crowded restaurant.

The perch was as good as advertised and so was the lemon meringue pie that finished off the meal. "Okay, five stars it is," he told her as they walked to his car. "The pie rivaled my grandmother's, not that I'd ever tell her."

After pulling onto the highway, he said, "In case you didn't notice, you were the sensation of the evening."

"Not as far as Kelly was concerned. By the way, did you notice both you and I wore black tonight?"

"Immediately. Had no idea I might have infected you with my color taste, but you can wear black for me anytime. I really—" He broke off, braking as a large black animal lumbered across the road in front of the car. "Damned if that's not a bear!"

"We do have those," she agreed. "Also deer, wolves and other assorted wildlife."

"In the woods, yes. It's just that I didn't expect to see a bear in the middle of the road."

"One never does—it's always a surprise when they show up at the farm searching for windfall apples or culls left on those old trees way out in back. Poor Fitzgerald. When he was still alive, he used to hide for days after he smelled a bear anywhere around. It was like he was saying, 'Hey, I'm a rabbit hound. I don't do bears.'"

"So tomorrow I'm going to be convincing your Scouts to plant apple seedlings for the eventual gratification of bears."

She laughed.

After he pulled into the farm driveway, he said, "My invitation still stands. I might add I do make a mean cup of coffee."

Rachel knew very well she ought to decline. She'd learned early to avoid situations that might turn into wrestling matches. If the man had been anyone but Mikel she would've said no, but somehow she trusted him not to try to rush her into anything she didn't want. Which was sort of scary, because she wasn't at all sure what she did want from him. Except, of course, to know who'd sent him here. Which was reason enough to accept his invitation.

"As for me, I'm perfectly harmless," he added as he parked the car.

How could he claim to be harmless with those green predator's eyes? "The better to see you with, my dear," she muttered without thinking.

"I didn't quite catch that."

She certainly wasn't going to admit she'd quoted the wolf's lines from Little Red Riding Hood. "Thank you, I'd love some coffee," she told him. "If you've done your homework, we can discuss tomorrow's Scout session while we drink it."

He opened the cottage door to usher her in. "If I think of anything I need to know, you'll be the first I'll ask."

"You sound pretty confident."

"That's the secret to coming out ahead."

Rachel thought about that as she seated herself in a chair near the fireplace. "Do you always come out ahead?" she asked finally.

He turned on the coffeemaker and sank down into the old chair on the opposite side of the fireplace. "Often enough to pay the bills."

"How about in the rest of your life?"

He shrugged. "We all make mistakes. I try not to repeat mine."

She'd just bet he usually succeeded, too. Hoping to work the conversation around to where he might reveal information she needed, Rachel said, "I've never actually met a private investigator before. What's it like being one?"

He sprang to his feet. "Forgot to light the fire." As he proceeded to do so, he spoke with his back to her. "A job is a job. If you're good at what you do and like it, then you stay interested. I imagine that's how you feel about teaching."

"More or less. But teaching students is rewarding in itself."

He rose and turned to her. "Catching bad guys can be, too."

"I'm sure. Do you think there's a bad guy in the case you're on now?"

"I don't yet have enough information to know one way or the other." He headed for the coffeemaker. "If that red light's any indication, the coffee's done. While we drink it, maybe you can help by telling me what you remember about Leo."

Rachel tensed. "You still think he was involved in the girl's disappearance?"

"I can't be positive one way or the other. I came here to find out."

"But he didn't have anyone but his wife and daughter with him when he came home to Ojibway."

"Apparently not. Still, that really only proves Renee Reynaud wasn't with him when he arrived here, not that he wasn't involved in some way." Having poured coffee into the two mugs he'd bought, he carried one to her, saying, "As I recall, you drink yours black."

She nodded, not really wanting to talk about Leo, but at the same time certain he'd wonder why, if she didn't. Trying to find a place to begin, she started with "Leo was a good teacher. He inspired both Eva and me to become teachers, too."

"Why was he good?"

"He was a quiet man who cared about children. He really listened to what they said to him and never turned a child away without the best answer he could find."

"You were fond of him."

It wasn't a question, but she responded, anyway.

"He was like a father to me—the right kind of father." After a moment she added, "Being an orphan, that meant a lot." She sipped the hot coffee and essayed a smile. "I thought maybe I was being invited into the wolf's den for an attempted seduction tonight, but I see I was wrong."

Mikel grinned at her. "Do you prefer being seduced? I always aim to please."

She wished he wouldn't look at her like that, his green eyes glowing as he let his gaze drift over her. She also wished it made her angry rather than making her wonder what it would be like if he kissed her. He had the most beautiful mouth, well-shaped and enticing.

"To be truthful, something like seduction did lurk in the back of my mind," he admitted.

"Well, at least you haven't lit any candles yet."

"So you prefer a romantic seduction? I'll keep it in mind."

"Actually, no. I happen to think candles and soft music is overkill."

"Then we're okay here?" He gestured toward the fireplace. "We at least have the warm fire, the eager male and the ambivalent female."

She laughed. "You make it sound like something out of Psych 101. Besides, how do you know I'm ambivalent? I might not have the least inclination to have you so much as hold my hand."

"Shall we find out?" Before she could answer, he set his coffee aside, came out of his chair, hauled the stool over and settled on it in front of her. Leaning against her legs, he reached for her hand and captured it. "How's that? Does it help your inclination one way or the other?"

The feel of him against her legs sent a tingle along her spine. As for his hand, warm and strong, curled around hers—okay, so she didn't want him to move away.

"The female finds she doesn't object to hand-holding." She managed to keep her tone light, when what she really wanted to do was purr.

"That being so, curtailing his eagerness, the male plans his next move, searching for an innocuous-seeming, unalarming but still erotic caress." He let go of her hand. "How about a foot massage?"

"I don't think...." But he'd already slipped off her boot and sock and her words trailed away as she felt his fingers gently kneading the ball of her foot. Never in her life had anyone massaged her feet. She sighed in pleasure, deciding not to refuse. After all, it was only a game they were playing and she could stop anytime she wished. To bare one foot certainly wasn't dangerous.

The next she knew she had two bare feet and she was thoroughly enjoying his magic touch. Better take care, she warned herself through her growing languor. She couldn't recall ever feeling so warm and relaxed and at the same time expectant, both wanting him to go on doing this forever and yet waiting for what would happen next. Which was madness.

But madness of such a sensual kind that she didn't seem to be able to make herself care. Whoever would think having a foot massage could lead to thoughts of further intimacy? Which was definitely happening. If she didn't watch out she'd be in over her head. She must do something, make some kind of stand now, before it was too late.

With an effort, Rachel forced herself to sit fully upright, pulling her feet away from Mikel and tucking them under her in the chair.

He smiled. "Going too fast, was I?"

"Yes. I mean, no. I just don't care to play the game anymore."

He rose and stretched, looking down at her. "The only real danger comes when it ceases to be a game, you know."

There was no way she intended to admit she'd already passed that point. While she watched him collect her empty mug, along with his own, and carry them over to the coffeemaker, she kept trying to come up with words to indicate her total disinterest in the subject. She couldn't seem to find anything appropriate, which annoyed her.

"I have to get home and see if there are any phone messages waiting," she said finally, as she bent to pull on her socks and boots. "The hospital might have tried to reach me."

He didn't comment, and when she was ready, he escorted her to the door.

"Thanks for the dinner," she told him. "And the coffee."

"My pleasure," he assured her. "It's not often Little Red Riding Hood comes to visit."

Damn the man, he'd caught what she'd meant earlier. Did he ever miss anything? Men like Mikel were dangerous, she had to keep that in mind at all times. "It's not often Little Red Riding Hood gets away from the Big Bad Wolf, either," she said.

"You flatter me."

She chuckled despite herself. "You know better. It really is time for me to say good-night. Please don't feel you need to escort me to my door. This is as close to a no-crime area as you can get."

She had to pass him to leave the cottage, and for a moment she paused looking into his eyes. Only when she glanced away was she able to ease past him and out the door, trying to keep her pace slow so it wouldn't look as though she were running away. Which she was. If she'd stayed a moment longer, she'd couldn't have trusted herself not to lift her face for the good-night kiss that waited for her there in those green eyes.

Mikel watched her from his open door until she reached the house, entered and shut off the outside light. So much for promising Aino to stay around to keep her safe. Rachel would be much safer with him miles away.

Closing the cottage door, he returned to the armchair, picking up the pamphlet of planting on the way. Never let it be said that, even though frustrated in other areas, a special agent doesn't do his homework.

In the morning it was breakfast at Sylvia's. He got Dottie with her aquamarine eyes as his waitress again. "Hear you and Rachel ate out at Metrovich's last night," she said.

He nodded, realizing there was little a person could do in this place without word getting around fast. "Good perch," he said. "Saw a bear on the way home, too."

"One of them Dumpster bears, probably. They hang around the restaurants outside of town."

Her words made him sorry he'd mentioned the bear. Somehow it took away the surprised pleasure he'd felt in seeing a wild animal. He ordered quickly.

When he finished eating, he took a turn on foot around the town, where he fell into conversation with a man walking a dog. When he finally worked the conversation as casually as he could past canines to Leo's return to Ojibway, the man, whose name was Don, shook his head.

"I went to school with Leo, but he wasn't much for talking, so I never knew him all that well. He was stuck on the Laati girl even then. She was real pretty but kind of sickly. My folks said she had some kind of chronic problem that'd kill her young, which I guess it did. No one was surprised when he brought her back here to die.''

"Just him and his daughter with her, no nurse or anyone else?''

Don shook his head. "No nurse. And Eva was too little to be much help. Good thing Aino and his wife took that orphan in when they did. Just in time, as it turned out.''

"Just in time?'' Mikel repeated.

"Yeah. Rachel got there no more than a day or so before Leo drove into town with his dying wife and his little girl. What he'd've done without Rachel to help out doesn't bear thinking about.''

After leaving Don, Mikel walked across the bridge to where boats were moored in a small marina. More than one local person had remarked on how lucky it was for Leo that Rachel had turned up when she did. He mistrusted coincidences, but chances were this was one, unless he was all wrong about Rachel's honesty—and he didn't think he was. Besides, even if she'd had red hair, she didn't really resemble the how-she-might-look-today computer picture he'd had made up from Renee's fourteen-year-old photo.

Ed at headquarters should have a file on Rachel Hill anytime now. He'd give him a call on Monday. Her file should eliminate the slightest possibility there was something more than coincidence here.

Mikel stopped by the village library to check out

a few details he wanted to know about tree planting, then finished up his other errands before heading back to the farm.

Shortly after lunch, girls began to arrive on bikes. Most looked to be between ten and twelve. He'd always thought of little girls as gigglers, but this group of eleven merely eyed him covertly as they gathered in the backyard and whispered among themselves. A guy in black jeans and T-shirt probably didn't remind them too much of Johnny Appleseed, but he wondered what they did think of him. Though sure of himself around women, this gaggle of girls put him on edge.

Hell, he'd never been around kids much. Back in Washington D.C., some of his buddies helped out with local boys' clubs and such, but he'd never gotten into it. As for little girls, the only one he'd had anything to do with was Steve's daughter, Heidi, and she was just a toddler. She was cute and fun to play with, but all she wanted from him was a piggyback ride or a push on the swing.

These Scouts expected much more. It'd be a snap to teach them how to safely handle a gun, for instance—he could do that in his sleep. But trees? Planting? What did he know?

Enough to fake it, he told himself. He might not be able to teach them what Aino would have, but he'd do it his way and let the flak fall where it may. At least it would keep his mind off Rachel and what had started to happen between them last night.

While he watched from the sidelines, which consisted of the seedlings in their pots, Rachel called the meeting to order, disposed rapidly of whatever business there was and then introduced him, explaining that Mikel Starzov was substituting today for Aino, who was still in the hospital, though he'd be home soon. When she finished, she gazed at Mikel expectantly. So did all the girls, who were now sitting on the grass.

He felt like a fool when he walked over and stood looking down at them, so he promptly sat down, too. "I know you've all heard about Johnny Appleseed," he began, "so I'm not going to read his story to you. Instead, I want each of you to tell me something about him." He pointed to his right, at the girl sitting at the end of the line. "We'll start here and go across to the end, then back along the second row. Tell me your name first, then a few words about our hero."

"I'm Delia," the towheaded girl said. "Johnny Appleseed was a man who traveled around a lot."

He smiled in approval and went on to the next girl. It went well, everyone contributing something, but was over far too quickly, making it his turn again.

"He may have been a bit eccentric, but all in all, he was a good man who furnished America with a tremendous amount of apples," he said in conclusion. "Though we're going to add a few more apple trees today, I want you to think about what would happen if all over the country Girl Scout Troops started planting apple seedlings. Since some variety or other of apple will grow almost anywhere, pretty soon the U.S. would be inundated with apples— right?''

"Um, I guess," Delia said.

"Apples are one of those things that, despite being healthy, taste good, but too many would be too many. So, what you need to do as Scouts is find other kinds of seedlings to plant where there are no trees but need to be. Each one of you on your own, not as a troop. We can't have too many trees, even if we can have too many apples. Today, though, we'll learn with apple seedlings, and when we get through, Aino's going to have a regular apple orchard here instead of just a few old trees out in back.''

He rose, saying, "I'll start off by planting the first one. I want you to know that, though I've read books and pamphlets about how to plant a tree, I've never actually done it. So we're learning together. Luckily we have Rachel here to set us right if we go wrong.''

He'd noticed most of the girls were now smiling, which he decided was a plus. But it wasn't until he'd dug his hole, explaining why it had to be larger than the seedling's immediate needs, that he began to relax. He then used the hose to fill the hole with water, letting it soak in before he carefully removed the seedling from its pot.

''Don't be afraid to get your hands dirty. Garden gloves are okay, but so are muddy hands.'' He waggled one of his mud-caked ones and heard someone giggle. He grinned, suddenly enjoying himself. When the little tree was in the hole, the dirt replaced and carefully tamped down, he eyed Delia. ''Guess who's next?'' he said to her. ''Choose your tree.''

By the time five trees were in, the girls were chattering to one another and to him, cheering when he viewed each planting critically before pronouncing it a masterpiece. After they were done and were washing their hands in the hose water, he said, ''Listen up. I talked to the Department of Natural Resources person and she's going to arrange to deliver pine seedlings to Rachel for you guys.

''The pine you get will be yours to plant where you think it needs to go. In your yard is okay, if your folks agree. Anybody else's yard, you need to get permission first. But there are lots of bare places on land owned by one government agency or another and guess what?''

''What?'' several voices chorused.

''They get mad if people cut down trees from their land, but they don't care if you plant one there.''

''They don't?'' Delia asked.

''Nope. I checked.''

Later, after cookies and soft drinks, Mikel stood in the drive with Rachel, watching the girls ride off on their bikes. Delia, who'd hung back, said to Rachel, "Probably Aino won't be all well yet by next week, so can Mikel come with us on our camp-out instead?"

Both Rachel and Delia looked at him.

"I'm willing, but that's up to your fearless leader," he told Delia.

Rachel nodded, saying, "If your parents all agree, that is."

Delia shouted, "Wait'll I tell the others," and pedaled as fast as she could down the driveway.

"You don't mind a camp-out?" Rachel asked.

"Just because I'm a city boy doesn't mean I don't know my way around a tent." Which was true. Part of agency training involved wilderness lore, which included camping with and without tents. "You haven't commented on today's performance," he added.

"It's one they'll remember, that's for sure."

He was about to ask if that was negative or positive when he noticed a red car pulling into the driveway. "Company's coming," he said.

Rachel frowned. "I don't recognize the car. I wonder who it can be?"

He watched it pull up close to them and stop. The door opened and a gray-haired woman stepped briskly out. "It can't be," he muttered. "Impossible."

She waved and started toward them. "I found you, Mikel! And there's Rachel, too. Oh, isn't she sweet. Of course, I knew she'd have to be, but seeing is believing.''

''Who is that?'' Rachel whispered. ''Do you know her?''

His sigh was heartfelt. ''I'm afraid so. She's my Grandmother Sonia.''

Chapter Five

Reaching Mikel, Grandma Sonia threw her arms around him. He hugged her, despite everything, glad to see her. Holding her away, he asked, "What are you doing here?"

She beamed. "Once you told me you'd found the right girl, I just knew I had to come, so I got on the Internet. That computer was the best present you ever bought me. Do you know I was able, on-line, to get plane reservations to a town near this out-of-the-way place and rent a car there so I could drive over? Remarkable! Then a nice young man at a gas station in Ojibway—Bob, his name was—told me where Rachel Hill lived. So here I am."

She turned to Rachel and held out her arms. He

watched as Rachel walked hesitantly toward her and was enveloped in a warm hug. "I just knew Mikel would find a nice girl someday," Sonia said as she released her.

Fervently regretting trying to placate his grandmother by telling a fib about why he was in the Upper Peninsula, Mikel tried to explain. "Actually Rachel and I are almost strangers. We—"

Sonia clapped her hands. "How wonderful. Love at first sight, just like with Boris and me. I know all about that."

"But we—" Michael began.

Sonia cut him off. "You can tell me all about it later, dear. Right now, I want to get better acquainted with this girl of yours." Looking at Rachel, she said, "Do you mind if we talk inside, dear? I really do need to freshen up."

Mikel watched Rachel's bemused expression change to one of polite concern. "Of course," she said. "Please do come in. I'm afraid you took me by surprise."

"I do love surprises," Sonia said as she followed Rachel toward the house, Mikel bringing up the rear. "Do you live with your parents, Rachel?"

"No. The house belongs to my cousin, Aino Saari."

"So he's Finnish? I'm Russian, you know."

As Rachel nodded, Mikel nipped ahead and opened the door, holding it for them.

"You know, this boy never lost the manners I

taught him," Sonia observed as she and Rachel entered the house. "That's more than you can say for many of the young men these days. Rude, that's what they are."

"There's no need to try to convince Rachel I'm a hot prospect," Mikel said. "The truth is—"

Sonia held up her hand. "Later, dear. I really must freshen up first." She looked expectantly at Rachel, who managed a smile and led her toward the stairs. As they left the room, Mikel threaded his fingers through his hair, gripping it, ready to howl in frustration. What a mess! With nobody to blame but himself. He'd never dreamed his grandmother would take it into her head to hunt him down. It was his own fault for forgetting she'd never been one to sit back and allow things to take their own course. She always knew a better way.

On the way upstairs, Rachel decided that, little as she understood why Sonia was here, common courtesy demanded she invite her to stay at the house. So she showed Sonia into a guest bedroom, saying, "There's a private bathroom through that door. I'll have Mikel bring up your suitcase."

"Thank you. I do hate to impose, but I simply couldn't sit around in my condo waiting once I knew Mikel had found the girl of his dreams."

Rachel blinked, more confused than ever. "He told you that?"

"Not in so many words, but he admitted you

were the reason he'd come to such an unusual place.''

Jolted, Rachel said, ''Me?''

Sonia nodded. ''Mikel tends to keep secrets. I'm sure he wouldn't have told me anything about the wonderful girl he'd met if I hadn't made him feel guilty for not coming to see me. Sometimes a pinch of guilt is worth a thousand scolds. Now, if you'll excuse me, dear...''

''Of course.'' Rachel headed for the door. ''I'll wait downstairs.''

She found Mikel pacing in the living room. He paused, giving her a rueful look. Before he could speak, she said, ''So I'm the girl of your dreams?''

His aghast expression made her chuckle.

''When I called Sonia my first day in Ojibway,'' he said, ''she asked me why I was here, and I didn't want to tell her anything about the case I was on so I fibbed a bit. I should have remembered liars always get tripped up sooner or later—sooner for me, as it turned out. Sonia tends to be unpredictable as well as inquisitive.''

Enjoying herself, Rachel said, ''Are you telling me I'm not the girl of your dreams? I'm crushed.''

He raised his eyebrows. ''Only time will tell, my proud beauty.'' Giving her a level look, he added, ''You're not upset by Sonia's arrival?''

''I think it's hilarious—the infallible P.I. brought low by his grandmother. As for her, she's an awesomely cool lady.''

He grinned, obviously relieved. "I agree, awesome but interfering."

"How do we…?" she began, pausing when she heard footsteps on the stairs. "I promised your grandmother you'd bring up her suitcase," she said.

Mikel shot out the door so fast Rachel had to laugh. How could she be angry when he'd got such a funny comeuppance?

Sonia came into the living room, glanced around and said, "Is your cousin Aino around? I'd like to meet him."

"Aino's in the hospital." Rachel went on to tell her what had happened, beginning with Mikel's opportune arrival and the events that followed. "The doctor says Aino may be coming home by tomorrow," she finished. "He'll have to have physical therapy for a while, though."

Sonia clapped her hands together. "How remarkable! Fate has surely taken a hand in this. From what you've told me, my dear Rachel, I can't help but believe I was sent here for a purpose. Mikel may not have told you, but I am a trained physical therapist and I can work right here at home with your cousin. That would save him trips to the hospital to have the therapy."

Somewhat taken aback, Rachel said, "That's very kind of you, but Aino will have to decide what he wants to do."

"How old a man is he?"

Trying to be tactful, since she had no idea how

old Sonia was, Rachel said, "A few years your senior, anyway."

Sonia nodded. "Then he'll take the suggestion better from me than from you. When I've rested, I'll have Mikel take me to visit him."

Seeing that Mikel's grandmother had a mind of her own equivalent to Aino's hardheadedness, Rachel decided it might be best to let the two of them confront each other rather than for her to get into the middle of a no-win situation.

"Would you like something to eat? A cup of coffee?" Rachel asked.

"A cup of tea would be welcome. I'll take it up to my room. A lovely room, by the way. I do enjoy old houses. They have such character."

Later, with Sonia upstairs with her hot tea and her suitcase, Rachel left the house, planning to go into town and visit Aino before supper. Mikel, sitting on the back porch, intercepted her.

"I keep trying to tell Sonia the truth," he said, "but she's like an eel, always slipping away."

"She probably doesn't want to hear it."

"That's likely. I overheard her offer to become Aino's therapist. Are you going to warn him?"

"I'll tell him your grandmother is visiting and will be coming to see him tonight with you. Let the two of them work it out."

He gave her a commiserating look. "I don't blame you. Sorry to have placed you in this awkward position."

Rachel found herself supporting him. "One you couldn't foresee."

"I should have, knowing my grandmother. I'll do what I can to try to talk her out of her decision."

"I suppose she really *is* a qualified physical therapist?"

"New York State says so, and until she retired, she earned a respectable income practicing it."

"I have this feeling Sonia will prevail, no matter what Aino's objections. She just ignores what she doesn't want to hear." Rachel sighed. "I sort of envy her the knack. Well, I'm off."

At the hospital, she found Aino prowling around his room without using the walker he'd been given. "Feel like a caged bobcat," he told her. "What I need is to be home."

"Tomorrow's not that far off," she countered, then told him to expect company after supper.

"Mikel's grandmother?" He scowled. "I'm expected to entertain some old biddy?"

"Sonia doesn't really fit into that category."

He grunted, obviously unconvinced. "You haven't told me how Mikel did with the Scouts."

"They want him to come on next week's campout, so I'd say he did okay."

"Start at the beginning."

So she did, which took her a while. By the time she finished, Aino was chuckling. "No flies on that boy."

Before she left, she told him she intended to call

Eva's friend in New York and leave a message there for Eva to call home. "She ought to know what happened to her grandfather, even if you are better."

He shrugged. Eyeing him, Rachel wished she could tell him straight out why Mikel had come to Ojibway, so she could share her unease with someone.

But that wouldn't be fair, considering he was still recuperating. She'd just have to wait until Eva called. Even then, there were some things about Mikel she couldn't share with Eva—or anyone else. The way he made her feel, for example.

When she returned home, Rachel discovered the table set and Sonia bustling about in the kitchen fixing beef stroganoff.

"You didn't have to cook supper," Rachel said.

Sonia smiled at her. "And why not? This I could make in my sleep."

"But you're a guest."

"Guests can't cook?"

Knowing when she was outflanked, Rachel subsided. "It's very good of you. I'll make a salad."

"That's done, dear. And I have peach cobbler in the oven. You go on and find Mikel."

"I do have a few chores to do," Rachel said hastily.

"Farm work is never done, as my own dear departed mother often said. Which was one of the reasons I left the old country. Now I find I miss the old ways—even gathering eggs. Do you have chickens?''

Rachel shook her head. "Not anymore. Just the cow.''

"A farm should have chickens. Nothing tastes the same as a really fresh egg.''

Wondering if their lives would ever be the same by the time Sonia left, Rachel escaped to the field where the cow grazed, then brought the animal back to the barn to be milked. Afterward she washed up and found Mikel helping his grandmother put the food on the table. Feeling like a visitor in her own home, Rachel let him seat her.

As she'd suspected, the meal was delicious. Though she'd known Sonia only for a matter of hours, Rachel was beginning to believe there was little Mikel's grandmother didn't do well. But, of course, she hadn't yet come up against Aino.

After they ate, Rachel insisted on doing the cleanup.

"So thoughtful of you, dear," Sonia said. "This way Mikel and I can get to the hospital early and make our visit short so we don't tire the poor man out.''

On the way to the hospital, Mikel did his best to get his grandmother to listen to him about Rachel.

"You don't have to explain," Sonia told him. "It doesn't matter whether you've known her for a day or for years. What attracts a man to a woman and a woman to a man doesn't depend on how long an acquaintance they've had.''

''You're missing the point,'' he said. ''I came up here on a case and—''

''So? Is there some law that says you can't meet a nice girl while you're on a case?''

''But that's just it. Rachel—''

Sonia sailed on. ''She's as smitten as you are, that's easy to see. She watches you constantly.'' Smiling, she added, ''And why not? All the Starzov men have been handsome devils.''

''She watches me?'' Mikel said, distracted for the moment.

''When you're not looking at her. I was quite amused at the table about the way the two of you try to pretend.''

''Just what do you imagine we're pretending about?''

''That you are not physically attracted to each other, of course. Really, Mikel, I am not blind. Nor stupid.''

Taken aback at her acuteness—he certainly did have visions of Rachel in his bed—he began to wonder if Sonia was also right about Rachel. What did she feel for him, if anything? Before he knew it, they'd arrived at the hospital and he still hadn't straightened out Sonia.

They found Aino sitting in a chair in his room. As Mikel was making introductions, Sonia approached the chair. Nodding to Aino, she said, "Your left side, is it?"

He glared at her.

"Now, now, no need for that," she scolded. "I'm a registered physical therapist and will be supervising your exercises."

"You're what?" he growled.

"I believe you heard me." Her tone was firm. "I don't coddle my patients. You know and I know what you need to do to recover as much as possible, and so we will work together getting you there."

Aino glanced at Mikel, who shrugged and admitted, "Grandma Sonia is a therapist."

"Of course I had no idea you even existed when I came to visit Mikel," Sonia said. "Call it serendipity. Naturally, as a guest in your home, I wouldn't think of charging you."

Aino's scowl faded. "No charge, hey? You any good?"

"Very good."

"Getting kind of old for it, I'd say."

Sonia gave him a speaking look. "Do I look decrepit?"

Aino leaned back in the chair, deliberately giving her a once-over. "Not so's a man can see," he admitted finally.

"I'll get my instructions from your doctor and talk to the hospital therapist before you leave tomorrow," she told him, the finality in her tone suggesting the matter was settled.

Mikel, expecting some kind of protest from Aino, was surprised when all he did was nod. But as they were saying their farewells, Aino got in what seemed to be the last word. "Mind you, Sonia Starzov, if there's one thing I can't stand it's a pushy woman."

Sonia, at the door, turned and smiled sweetly. "Isn't it fortunate, then, Aino Saari, that I'm not one?"

Even-steven, Mikel decided as they drove back to the farm. Sonia chattered all the way, commenting on everything they passed, not giving him a chance to get a word in edgewise.

As he helped her from the car at the farm, she said, "I'd dearly love to take a short stroll in this marvelous northern twilight. Do run in and ask Rachel to join us."

At that moment, Rachel came around the corner of the house. "I was sitting on the back porch and heard you drive up. Where would you like to walk?"

"Oh, just a turn around the outside of the house—to help me sleep, you know," Sonia told her.

They set off, Sonia in the middle, telling Rachel about the visit with Aino. "He promises to be an interesting patient," she finished.

Mikel and Rachel looked at each other. "*Interesting* seems a mild word," Mikel remarked.

"I find it a useful one." Sonia stopped and

pointed. "Those seem to be the stairs to the back porch. I do believe it's time for me to call it a day."

All three climbed up to the porch. "I'm sure you two have things to talk about," Sonia told them. "I'm used to fending for myself so I'll just say good-night now." She opened the inside door and disappeared into the kitchen.

Mikel glanced at Rachel, "Let's sit down before we get into our 'things.'"

He motioned toward the porch swing.

When they were seated, gently gliding back and forth, Rachel said, "Your grandmother is one of a kind."

"Like Aino?"

She nodded. "You realize she left us alone on purpose. Which means you haven't told her the truth yet."

He sighed. "She doesn't make that easy." Leaning back, he gazed at the darkening sky where stars were beginning to be visible and listened to the piping of tree frogs. "This is a peaceful spot."

"You sound as though you don't get much of that."

"You're right." His arm, lying along the back of the swing, brushed against her hair, a casual-enough contact. Why, then, could he feel it all the way down to his toes? He turned toward her. "Rachel, look at me."

He'd meant to say something about—what? When her gaze met his, all thought vanished. Bending his head, he found her lips, warm and soft and so enticing he wrapped his arms around her to hold her closer. Caught up in a fiery burst of need, he deepened the kiss, tasting her sweetness and feeling her eager response.

The heat built between them until he was no longer aware of the evening sounds. He lost contact with where he was, the only reality was Rachel, here in his arms, infinitely desirable. He wanted more, wanted all of her.

Rachel had never felt so thoroughly kissed. Mikel's taste became a potent lure, urging her on, making her press closer and closer to him. Nothing that felt this wonderful could be wrong, it wasn't wrong to let herself go, to reach out for what she needed so desperately. He was what she'd always wanted but couldn't have. This time she'd forget everything, everything except Mikel....

Chapter Six

As they sat entwined together on the porch swing, Mikel's hands, warm and caressing, slipped under her T-shirt to cup her breast and she made an involuntary sound of pleasure.

"Rachel," he murmured against her lips.

The sound of her name brought her out of her erotic daze, reminding her that she didn't dare to let herself go, not with anyone—and especially not Mikel. Though she wanted so badly to stay in his arms, she forced herself to push him away. "No," she said hoarsely, "I can't."

There was no explanation she could give him. Getting up, she fled into the house and up to her bedroom, where she sat on the edge of her bed, trying to dispel the emotions he'd aroused. No, the emotions she'd allowed him to arouse in her. Tears blurred her eyes, forcing her to remove her contacts. She hugged herself, letting the tears run down her cheeks, holding to her lifelong habit of not making a sound. Crying showed weakness and she'd always had to be strong. When the tears did come, anyway, it was best to get it over with quietly, so no one knew.

Why couldn't she be like any other woman? She was, inside. If she'd ever doubted it, tonight had proved she was. But, to her, making love with a man meant losing control of herself and that was something she couldn't afford to do. And Mikel was the last man in the world she could take such a risk with, no matter how right it had felt to be in his arms.

Never before had she felt so devastated by the decision she'd made when she was nineteen and imagined herself in love with that jerk Tim Thompson. One night, after belatedly realizing she didn't dare open herself emotionally to anyone, she'd told him to stop, that she couldn't make love with him.

Tim hadn't taken it well, first trying to force her and then, when she fought back, calling her frigid before stalking off and never speaking to her again. How hurt and disillusioned she'd been. Though she'd been careful not to get into a similar position again, she couldn't say she'd ever had a close relationship with any man. How was it possible considering her situation?

Rachel wiped her eyes and went into the bathroom to wash her face. Maybe it was a good thing Sonia had arrived when she did. Mikel's grandmother would be a buffer between her and him. She'd encourage Sonia to stay on until Mikel was satisfied the lost girl wasn't to be found here. Then he'd leave and everything would go back to normal.

Normal. That thought almost reduced her to tears again.

Mikel sat on the swing until he'd cooled off a bit—those hot kisses they'd exchanged had sent him up too damn high for comfort—then he left the porch and walked around the yard. He noticed a light in the upstairs room he knew was Sonia's, then saw the light go on in Rachel's bedroom. He took a deep breath and released it slowly.

Slowly, yes, that was the right path. Don't rush anything. Even if she had given every indication she wanted what he wanted.

The wisest move would be to back off completely. Romancing her was not a good idea, considering. He headed for the cottage. Between coping with Sonia's unexpected arrival and his yen for Rachel, he'd slacked off. Tomorrow he'd return to the hunt. It was, after all, why he was here.

In the morning, Mikel turned on the coffeemaker, then showered and dressed. He sat down to drink the first cup, planning out his day with a lack of enthusiasm that troubled him. When someone knocked on the cottage door, he leaped up. Rachel? When he opened the door, his grandmother stood there.

"Breakfast is ready," she announced. "I'm glad to see you're up and dressed because Aino will be fretting if we don't show up early to bring him home."

Mikel, who'd forgotten Aino was being discharged from the hospital today, realized he'd have to rearrange his own plans because he was obviously the one who should be there to give what help was needed. Also, if Sonia was going to continue to make meals, then he needed to go with her to buy groceries. With both of them camping out at the farm, they had to contribute. Rather than being annoyed at postponing what he'd planned, he found himself whistling as he walked with Sonia over to the house.

"You must be feeling good if you're whistling one of the old Russian folk tunes I taught you," she said.

"What?"

"You're whistling *Dark Eyes.*"

So he was. And thinking of Rachel, with her soft brown eyes, waiting inside the farmhouse. Which was not a good start to backing off.

When they got Aino home—using Sonia's rental

car because it was a full-size four-door—Mikel helped him into the house.

"You going to get this arm and leg of mine back to normal, Sonia Starzov?" Aino asked.

Sonia, walking ahead of them, turned to say, "That depends on you and whatever higher power you believe in."

"Humph. What'd Doc tell you?"

"The same as he told you. The leg may come all the way back, the arm may improve."

"He's cagey, Doc is."

"He also told me you were lucky to be getting your own private therapist since they're short-handed at the hospital right now."

"We'll see about that."

Rachel glanced at Mikel with raised eyebrows and he smiled at her. He wasn't worried about Aino and Sonia getting along. When he had a chance, he'd tell her how Sonia and his grandfather had enjoyed bickering.

Once inside, Sonia said, "Where do you want to do the exercises?"

"The back porch," Aino told her.

"Fine, weather permitting. We'll start after you rest a bit."

"I'm not going to bed and that's final," Aino roared.

"Don't argue with your therapist. And who said anything about bed? You can rest on the porch swing."

Grumbling, Aino walked slowly through the kitchen to the door leading to the porch. Watching him, Rachel saw that he didn't limp exactly, but his left leg dragged a bit. She bit her lip, knowing how he must hate the impairment. Sonia followed him out onto the porch, closing the door behind her.

"Grandma's not easily fazed," Mikel said.

"So I see." Rachel had hardly been able to look at him this morning and she didn't now. Spotting the note lying on the kitchen table, she picked the paper up and waved it at him. "This is Sonia's grocery list. She said to give it to you, but I can easily—"

"No way. I'll go."

"But I need to get groceries myself. I'd be happy to—"

"We'll go together." He grinned at her. "Don't argue with your guest."

Rachel relaxed a little, smiling despite herself. Okay, so she was overwhelmingly attracted to him physically, but she also liked Mikel. He was easy to be with. She might even be able to trust him, if there wasn't this barrier preventing her from ever trusting anyone except the Saaris. Mikel, especially, had to be kept outside that barrier.

In the grocery store, they ran into Bob from the gas station. "Did that lady in the red car get to your place okay?" he asked Rachel.

"Yes, thanks for helping her."

"Friend of yours?"

"She's my grandmother," Mikel explained.

"Aino getting on all right?" Bob asked.

"Yes," Rachel said. "We brought him home from the hospital this morning."

"Glad to hear it. Well, see you two around."

Mikel, who'd already decided the village information pipeline was more efficient than the Internet, figured that, by tonight, everyone in town would know Sonia was Aino's private physical therapist. If he could find a way to tap into this community knowledge without raising suspicions by asking too many questions, he had a hunch he might be able to piece enough together to discover whether or not Leo Saari had some covert connection with Renee's disappearance.

On the surface, it appeared Leo did not, but surfaces were often deceptive.

In the checkout line they encountered a mother of one of the Scouts. "Laurie says the camp-out is still on," she said to Rachel, giving Mikel sidelong glances. "I thought maybe with Aino having had the stroke and all, you might postpone it, but I'm glad you called me to say your guest will be taking Aino's place. Laurie will be so disappointed if she can't go."

"She meant me," Mikel said.

"Oh, you must be the man who's getting the pine trees from the Department of National Resources for the girls to plant," the woman said.

Rachel broke in to introduce them. "As I mentioned, Mikel and his grandmother are staying at the farm with us,'' she added.

"How nice," Laurie's mother said. "You'll let me know for sure about the camp-out, then?"

Rachel nodded.

After putting the groceries in the car, Mikel said, "Which is the best way to get closer to Lake Superior? I've only had glimpses of it so far."

"There's a township park along the lake," she said. "I'll show you where to turn."

"A park? Good." He meant to force a discussion of last night and they needed to be alone, preferably not driving in a car. He intended to stop so they could get out and stroll along the beach.

When he finally pulled into a small parking lot and turned off the engine, he said, "Game to go wading?"

She stared at him. "Have you ever waded in this lake?"

"No, that's why I suggested it. Something wrong about doing that?"

"Of course not." Rachel bent to remove her shoes. "I was surprised that you wanted to."

"Because I'm a city boy? As a kid I swam in the Atlantic."

Leaving their shoes and socks in the car, they walked through a cluster of huge old white pines toward the water. The day was warm and the sun glinted off lazy waves pushing up onto golden-brown sand. Mikel gazed out at the blue water stretching to the horizon with no land in sight, and something within him responded to the uncluttered beauty of the scene.

"No boats out there," he said. "And no one on the beach." He looked at her questioningly.

Rachel pointed. "See that line of dark clouds just above the horizon?"

"Doesn't look like much of a threat to me."

"That's because you didn't grow up on this lake. Nobody's taken a boat out because they know in about an hour, the wind'll be up, causing waves you won't believe, with the worst of the storm still to come. Since mothers don't generally bring their kids to the beach until afternoon and most teenagers are either working or sleeping till noon, that's why nobody's here."

He grinned at her. "We are. Race you to the water."

She stopped short of getting her feet wet, but he splashed in, immediately splashing right out again. "Straight from the Arctic," he complained as he began to walk with her alongside the water.

"Forty-five degrees," she said, smiling.

"You didn't warn me."

"You didn't ask."

Seeing his opening, he said, "If I ask you about last night, will you be honest?"

Though he wasn't touching her he could sense her tensing. She didn't reply for so long he was beginning to think she might not, when she finally spoke.

"I shouldn't have let that happen."

"But you enjoyed it as much as I did." No question, he knew she had.

"Even so."

Honest Rachel. He quelled his impulse to hug her, knowing that would be unacceptable right now. "Then why shouldn't you have let it happen?" he asked.

"I don't care to discuss why."

He stopped, reached out and grasped her shoulders, turning her to face him, gazing directly into her eyes, noticing for the first time that she wore contacts. Which had nothing to do with the moment. "There's a list of excuses you could pick and choose among—you don't want an affair, I'm a stranger, it wasn't the right time or the right place— but you didn't use any of them."

She looked back at him without expression. "I don't need excuses. My reasons are my own. And private. There won't be another occurrence."

Though frustrated with her, he was in complete control of himself until her last few words made him feel she'd thrown down a gauntlet, challenging him. "Oh, won't there?" he muttered, and pulled her closer, his mouth coming down hard on hers. He meant the kiss to be brief, no more than an answer to her challenge, but once she was in his arms, he couldn't let her go. He wanted this woman more than he ever recalled wanting any other.

Rachel's first impulse to thrust him away faded and vanished as heat rose in her to answer the passion in his kiss. If only this could last forever. If only there were just the two of them involved. If only she had no past. How she longed to give way to her own desire, to melt into his arms.

Why did it have to be this man, of all men, who evoked such a deep, yearning need she didn't dare satisfy? She must break the spell of his kiss, she must pull free—and yet she couldn't make herself do what she knew had to be done.

A child's voice startled them both. "Mama, look—that man is kissing that lady just like on TV."

Rachel and Mikel broke apart abruptly. Neither had been aware until now that they were no longer alone on the beach. Rachel's face burned as she recognized the mother of one of her Scouts. The woman was holding the hand of a preschool child.

"Uh, hello, Mrs. Hansen," she said feebly.

"Lovely day, isn't it?" Mikel chimed in. "Too bad it's going to storm later."

He crouched down until he was even with the little boy. "Men do kiss ladies sometimes," he confided, "but only if they like them."

The boy blinked, taken aback by the attention from a stranger.

Mikel rose, nodded to Mrs. Hansen, who had yet

to say a word, grasped Rachel's hand and pulled her with him, back the way they'd come. Only when they reached the car did he release her.

"I don't know whether to thank you for getting me out of there so fast or be mad because you got us into that position to begin with," she said.

"Nice of you to be fair about it. My only excuse is I couldn't help myself. If you challenge me in the future, you'd best be prepared for the consequences."

Challenge him? What was he talking about? Then she recalled saying something to the effect that what had happened between them last night wouldn't happen again. Apparently he'd taken that as a challenge.

"I suppose you know word will be all over town in a flash," she told him.

He nodded. "Probably even before we get back to the farm." After he opened the car door for her, then got in himself, he added, "Surely, in this day and age, it won't affect your teaching position."

"Actually, I'm taking a sabbatical this coming school year to finish getting my master's degree, so it doesn't matter. Eva's going to substitute for me while I'm gone." She knew she was babbling nervously but couldn't seem to stop. "I'm not positive I'll be coming back to the same position afterward, but I'm sure I could if I wanted to. It's not the old days when a single female teacher couldn't even date without her morals being questioned. Though people *will* talk because the village is so small. It really doesn't matter to me.''

She had more difficult problems to worry about. How could she be upset at gossip when Mikel's mere touch kept her in such turmoil?

They were almost to the farm when he asked, ''So are we on for the overnight camp-out or not?''

No! rose to her lips, but she held it back. She couldn't disappoint the girls, who for weeks had looked forward to the hike and camp-out. With no reason not to go—Sonia would certainly take good care of Aino—she had little excuse to cancel. If only Delia hadn't asked if Mikel could come, it'd be simple. She and the girls could go by themselves.

''It's not really necessary for you to tag along,'' she said.

''Aino worries about you. Isn't that why he intended to go with you? You know he'll feel better if I take his place.''

She could hardly tell him Aino was one thing and he was quite another so she shrugged and said, as indifferently as she could manage, ''If you want to go to all that trouble. It won't be very exciting, after all.''

''Who needs excitement? I expect to enjoy myself. Peacefully.''

Damn the man. ''Well, all the mothers did agree. Be ready early Wednesday morning,'' she said reluctantly.

As she'd predicted, by the time they'd finished carrying in the groceries, the wind had picked up and dark clouds were rapidly covering the sky. Grandma Sonia was making chicken soup for lunch, while Aino rested on the couch in the TV room.

"Your cousin is very motivated," Sonia said to Rachel. "That makes him easy to work with. Of course that doesn't necessarily mean he's easy to get along with. What was his wife like?"

Actually, Rachel hadn't known Aino's wife Mary for very long before she died. Casting her mind back, she said, "Mary was quiet, she didn't talk much. But she was a kind woman."

"Quiet," Sonia said. "Yes, Aino would choose a quiet one."

"Grandpa Boris didn't," Mikel remarked. When Sonia waved the soup ladle threateningly at him, he added, "Time for me to head for the cottage."

"Be sure you're back here promptly at noon for lunch," Sonia warned him. "I don't cook for tardy people."

As soon as he was out the door, Sonia looked at Rachel. "How is everything going?" she asked.

"Everything?" Rachel echoed, knowing full well what Sonia meant.

"Has he confessed his feelings yet?"

"I'm not sure you understand exactly what the situation is," Rachel said.

"Who couldn't understand? The question is, when will he do something about it?"

Like making love to me on the porch swing? Rachel was tempted to say. "I think Mikel needs to talk to you about this," she told Sonia.

"Oh, that isn't necessary, not at all. I approve. You're the kind of girl I was always trying to find for him and I'm so happy he discovered you on his own."

"Thank you, but it's not exactly the way you might think."

Sonia's eyebrows rose "It's not? Don't you like my Mikel?"

"I like him fine." Rachel searched for words to try to explain without revealing what Mikel still hadn't managed to tell Sonia. It was up to him to do so—and the sooner the better.

"Then everything will work out—just you wait and see."

The ache in her chest told Rachel nothing could ever work out the way she wanted it to. "What can I help you with?" she asked Sonia, hoping to change the subject.

"You, who've already milked the cow, turned her out to feed, helped get Aino home, bought groceries and hauled them home, all before lunch? Let me putter on my own, I do best alone in the kitchen."

More or less turned out of her own kitchen, Rachel peeked in to check on Aino and saw he was sleeping. She wandered into his bedroom—the only one downstairs—and saw that Sonia had already put everything away that he'd brought back from the hospital. Rachel might have felt resentful, but she liked Sonia and realized the older woman must be lonely and welcomed the chance to feel useful again. If only things were different and there was a chance that Mikel…

But Rachel had used up all her if-onlys long ago.

Chapter Seven

On Tuesday, Mikel called headquarters from a pay phone in town, hoping Ed, his contact, had something for him on Rachel Hill. He had little doubt she was who she claimed to be, but it'd be good if the agency confirmed the fact.

"What do you mean you hit a snag?" he demanded after a moment.

After listening some more, he said, "A gap in her records? What does that mean?"

"Maybe nothing," Ed told him. "I'm keeping on it. Call back in a week, give or take a few days."

Mikel thought about this as he returned to the farm, finally deciding not to let it bother him since the researcher didn't seem to think it was important.

But he did make up his mind to try again to get Sonia alone so he could straighten her out about his relationship with Rachel. He found her on the porch with Aino, both of them seated on the swing.

"My Mary was a sweet woman," Aino was saying. "Never raised her voice to me, unlike someone I could mention."

"That might have been fine for Mary," Sonia told him, "but I never had any ambition to be called sweet. I've always felt that if I don't speak my mind, who'll do it for me? Just because you were married to a quiet woman is no reason to expect the rest of us to keep our mouths shut. In any case, you're a stubborn man who needs prodding."

"Danged if I mean to let some mouthy female run my life."

"I'm trying to help you, not run your life," Sonia said. At that point she looked around and saw Mikel. "There you are," she exclaimed. Nodding toward the backyard, she added, "Rachel needs help airing out the tent."

Mikel left the porch to join Rachel. Once they had the tent under control, she asked, "Do you have a sleeping bag with you? If not, we have an extra."

"Always keep one in the trunk. Never know when it might come in handy."

"Good. How about a backpack?"

"Wouldn't be without one. I take it this'll be a fairly easy hike on a marked trail tomorrow."

She nodded.

"That tent looks like it sleeps two," he said.

Frowning, she said, "Not on this overnight trip."

"What if it rains?"

"It won't. But if it did, one of the girls could share it with me and you could use her one-man tent. Are you worried about sleeping in the open?"

"Wouldn't be my first time." Although he wasn't, strictly speaking, a camper, all the agents had to complete a course in wilderness survival, so he wasn't exactly a novice. Of course, he hadn't brought any of his special gear to the U.P. with him, but who'd need that on an easy hike on a marked trail?

Since the walk along the lake, Rachel had treated him with a you-might-be-a-friend-but-don't-get-too-close casualness. He supposed her attitude was just as well, even if he'd prefer a tad more intimacy. Better yet, a lot more. Which he wasn't likely to get on a hike with five Girl Scouts—that was all who were able to come. They were good kids and he liked them, but when what he really wanted was to be alone with Rachel, even one Scout was too many.

He tried, but found it impossible, to take Sonia aside before it was time to retire to the cottage for the night. The explanation would have to wait until he got back from the camp-out. As he settled into bed, remembering Rachel's rundown of the wild critters one might encounter up here, he decided to take along his gun, just in case. No one would notice it tucked away in his shoulder holster.

Using a van lent to Rachel by one of the girl's family, the five Scouts plus Mikel and Rachel reached the point of departure for the hike well before noon. Once the van was parked everyone collected their gear and scrambled out. Rachel did a final check to make sure nothing was forgotten.

"Okay, gang, backpacks secure and comfortable?" she asked. "Everybody got their whistles? Good. I'll take the lead, the five of you will follow with Mikel as rear guard."

"In case a wild animal sneaks up on us?" Delia asked.

Mikel was about to reassure her when he realized, by the giggles, that Delia was joking. Apparently these girls didn't take the possibility seriously. And they were probably right. Most wild critters were smart enough to keep as far away from humans as possible.

"Well, we could meet a porcupine," Beth said. "Nothing scares them."

"So we let him have the right of way," Rachel said. "Everyone clear on that?"

They were.

"What don't we do on the trail?" Rachel asked.

"Stray off," Carol said.

"Good. What else?"

"We don't eat," Laurie said.

"Right. Food might attract a bear."

"No litter," Beth said.

"Or tripping over stuff 'cause we aren't paying attention," Amy added.

"I'm beginning to think I've got the smartest Scout troop in the country," Rachel told them.

"We don't dig up any plants 'cause we're on a state park trail." Delia smiled at Mikel. "If we'd brought a tree, though, we could plant it."

"Good thinking," he told her.

When they set off, Mikel noticed that Delia had shuffled herself around so she was the last one in the line of Scouts, making him realize she wanted to be next to him. For some reason this made him feel as good as when he'd finished a case successfully.

He wasn't sure he was entirely happy about this—what was happening to his Nemesis persona?

Noise wasn't a no-no on the trail, he discovered. The Scouts sang, chattered and generally let every creature in the woods know they were coming. Other than a chipmunk streaking across the trail and into the safety of a decaying log, Mikel didn't see any other critters.

When they reached the campsite Rachel had chosen, everybody threw off their backpacks. Mikel saw it was no more than a small clearing in the otherwise dense woods.

"Can we eat now?" Beth asked.

"Not until the tents are up," Rachel told her.

"We'll put them over there near that grove of pines so we'll be off the trail." She pointed. Then, looking at Mikel, she warned, "No fair helping anyone—they have badges to earn."

He watched the girls, all of whom seemed to know what they were doing. But then, he already knew Rachel would be good at anything she undertook—teaching included. He glanced at her and their gazes locked for a moment until she blinked and looked away.

He took a deep breath and let it out, wondering what he was going to do about Rachel. She'd moved into his head, crowding out thoughts of what he should be doing instead of wanting to be with her. Covertly watching her, he didn't realize at first that Delia was trying to get his attention. He walked over to where she'd set up her tent.

Delia pointed to the pine grove. "She went in there."

"Who? What are you talking about?"

Glancing at Rachel, who was some distance away, Delia lowered her voice to a near whisper. "Laurie told me yesterday she was going to sneak into the woods and use her compass to get back to the camp just to prove she could. And she did."

"Maybe she just had to use the facilities," he pointed out.

"No, Rachel makes us go in pairs for that. Laurie's my friend but she likes to show off. I'm scared she might get lost and I don't want to tell Rachel on her 'cause then Laurie'll be in trouble. Can you go after her?''

Looking into Delia's trusting blue eyes, he nodded. It'd only take him a few minutes to find Laurie and haul her back to camp. Taking care not to be obvious, he sauntered toward the pines and slipped among the trees. Not until he was well into the woods did it occur to him that he didn't have a compass, something he'd always relied on in the agency tests. He shrugged. The camp wasn't far, surely he couldn't miss finding it again. Just in case, he tried to spot landmarks but, unfortunately, all the trees looked pretty much alike.

Pulling his all-purpose utility tool from his pocket—something he always carried—he used the knife part to carve a blaze into the trunk of one of the trees.

Okay, so you can find your way back here if you keep marking trees as you go on, he told himself. The problem is, can you be sure of the way back from here?

A shriek from somewhere up ahead froze him in place. Laurie! What had happened to her? He automatically touched his shoulder holster.

''Where are you?'' he called, hoping she'd be able to respond.

The high-pitched blast of a whistle answered him and he followed the sound until he finally caught sight of the yellow neckerchief all the girls wore.

''Laurie?''

"Here I am." Her words came out between sobs. He found her huddled against a pine trunk, crying.

"What happened?" he demanded.

She pointed up at a nearby cedar. "He climbed up there."

He looked but could see nothing through the foliage. "Who or what did?"

"The porcupine." She scrabbled in a pocket and came up with a wrinkled tissue, using it to wipe her eyes. "I didn't see him in time and—look." She thrust out one leg and he saw what were unmistakably quills stuck into her jeans at thigh level.

"It hurts," she wailed.

"Hold still," he ordered, flipping out the pliers part of the tool. He knelt on one knee. "It'll hurt worse for a little bit," he warned, "and then you'll feel better. There's no more than about five quills here so you got off pretty easy, considering. If you feel like it, you can scream when I pull them out."

Keeping up a running commentary to distract her, he began to extract the quills one by one. Laurie flinched and whimpered while he worked, but didn't cry out.

"Got 'em all," he said when he was through. "When we get back to camp Rachel will put antiseptic on them and you'll be okay. Think you can walk?"

She nodded.

"One little problem remains," he said. "Did you, by any chance, look at your compass before you left camp so you know what direction we should take?''

''I dropped it when the porcupine swiped me,'' she confessed.

''Where?''

''There, I think.''

After searching, Mikel finally came up with the shiny aluminum compass. ''We'll look at it together and you can tell me in which direction camp is.''

''West. It's west.''

He took her hand, and in what seemed no time at all, they reached the pine grove near the camp and soon came out among the tents.

''Thank heaven you found her!'' Rachel cried. ''We heard the whistle and then Delia told me what was going on. When I found out you'd gone after her, I decided to wait rather than make a search myself.''

Her trust in him warmed his heart, but he covered it by saying, ''Because I always get my man—or in this case, girl?''

''It was awful,'' Laurie said, beginning to cry again. ''Mikel had to pull five porcupine quills out of my leg and it really, really hurt. I wish I hadn't gone off alone.''

Mikel put his hand on her shoulder. ''Laurie was brave about it all. And here's my confession—if she hadn't looked at her compass before leaving camp, so she knew how to get back, we'd be out there yet blowing her whistle and waiting to be rescued. Because, you see, I went off without a compass. Never a good idea.''

Rachel, impressed by his admission that he, like Laurie, had made a mistake, also noticed how Laurie's tears had stopped when he called her brave. What a great guy he was. ''Come with me into my tent,'' she ordered Laurie. ''We'll get some antiseptic on that leg.''

When she and Laurie emerged, the other girls were gathered around Mikel, who, from the sound of their laughter, was evidently telling them a funny story.

Later, after the cookout, Mikel supervised the burying of the scraps of leftover food at a good distance from the camp, causing much amusement by instructing every one of the cleanup crew to check their compasses because otherwise he'd surely get lost again.

He was so different from the man she'd at first believed him to be, Rachel told herself. She would never have imagined the tough P.I. with the green hunter's eyes could care about her girls, their feelings as well as their welfare. No wonder Delia was suffering from an acute case of hero worship. Laurie probably would be, too, now. She couldn't blame them.

In the twilight, as they donned light jackets against the cool of the evening and began to gather around the campfire, Delia came up to Rachel and whispered something. Rachel bent to hear. "Carol says she heard her mother tell her father that Mikel kissed you on the beach," Delia confided. "Did he?"

Rachel sighed and tried to choose her words carefully, but wound up admitting, "Yes, he did."

"Are you going to marry him?"

Poor Delia, she probably wanted Mikel to wait until she got old enough so he could marry her. "No, we aren't going to marry," she assured the girl. "We're just friends."

Delia eyed her doubtfully, but then Rachel saw her notice how the other girls had begun to gather around Mikel. Delia immediately rushed over and made certain she got to sit next to him at the fire.

Then it was time for tales and songs and, eventually, bed. Once the girls were snug in their tents and quiet, Rachel came back to the fire and to Mikel, who was standing there staring into the flames. "I haven't had a chance to tell you how wonderfully you handled the porcupine episode," she said. "I had no idea Laurie would go off like that."

"Laurie was no more foolish than I," he said. "I hope you didn't scold her too much."

"No need. She learned a lesson without scolding."

"So did I," he said ruefully. "Not good to go around thinking you're infallible."

She smiled, looking into his eyes. "I'm glad you came on the hike."

He took her hands in his. "So am I."

What she wanted to do was sway toward him, into his arms, where he'd kiss her until the world went away and left them alone together. But they weren't alone. She pulled away. "It's time I crawled into my sleeping bag," she told him.

"I'll walk you home."

Since her tent was only a few yards away, it made no sense, but, wanting to prolong the moment, she said nothing. Side by side they walked to where her tent nestled among those of the girls. When they reached it, he took her arm and led her around to the back of the tent.

"I wouldn't want your Scouts to go home with tales of their fearless leader kissing the rear guard," he said.

"Carol has already told Delia about us on the beach. Delia wanted to know if we were getting married. I told her no, but I'm not sure she believed me. I think she intends to marry you herself."

"She's a cute kid. I hate to disappoint her, but marriage is definitely not my line."

"Nor mine."

He tipped up her chin with his forefinger. "Why not?"

"I don't care to discuss my reasons."

His lips came closer and closer, until she felt the

caress of his warm breath and he murmured, ''Tell me you don't want me to kiss you good-night.''

''No,'' she whispered, unsure whether she meant no, she didn't want him to, or no, she wasn't going to tell him anything of the sort.

Whatever she meant, he kissed her, anyway, and a thrill shot through her. She leaned into his embrace, sliding her hands under his open jacket. Bemused by this kiss, at first she didn't realize what was under one of her hands. Leather? When it finally occurred to her she must be touching a shoulder holster, she flung herself away from him.

''A gun!'' she cried. ''You're carrying a gun!'' She turned and fled around her tent and dived through the opening, pulling the flap closed. Crouched on her sleeping bag, she hugged herself, shuddering, fighting off the terror of the past.

Mikel stared after her in bewilderment. There was no mistaking her fright—his gun had given her a case of the blue devils. Just as, he remembered, his speaking of a gun had seriously troubled her once before. As he walked away from her tent toward the fire, he puzzled over her extreme reaction. Though she didn't know what he actually did for a living, she did believe he was a P.I., so the fact that he owned a gun shouldn't have been a surprise. What was it, then?

What had happened to Rachel in the past that even the bare mention of a gun frightened her? She lived in an area of the country where hunting was common. He suspected most of the men in Ojibway owned rifles and shotguns for hunting. Perhaps even Aino did.

He could ask Aino about Rachel's gun phobia. And, when he finally cornered Sonia and told her the truth about why he'd come to the U.P., he'd find out from her if she thought Aino was well enough to be asked the other questions that needed answering, about Leo and the missing Renee.

His obsession with Rachel was scattering his wits. He had to come to terms with it and get back to work on his mission. If she ever let him make love with her, that might do the trick, might rid him of this consuming need.

He wasn't looking for any long-term involvement with a woman. How could he after Yolanda had shattered his belief in any woman's honesty? True, Rachel did seem honest, but so had Yolanda. What he needed from Rachel was only a temporary coming together; it had to be that and no more.

Mikel sat down on his sleeping bag by the fire and stared into the dwindling flames as if they held the answers he needed.

Chapter Eight

After their return to the farm, while Rachel went off to deliver the van to Amy's parents and collect her own car from them, Mikel found his chance to corner his grandmother for a private conversation.

"This is truth-telling time," he confessed, once they were settled in the living room. "What I told you on the phone about Rachel wasn't true. I'd barely met her at the time. She's not my girl, I just said so to keep you from asking questions. Because I *am* on a case, even though I'm on vacation."

She frowned. "How can the people you work for do such a thing to you?"

"They didn't. This is my case, one not for pay. You remember meeting my friend Steve, well, it's a wedding gift to him.'' He went on to explain how Steve's bride, Victoria, had been devastated as a child when her older sister, Renee, had vanished. Renee had never been found.

"That was fourteen years ago and the trail's pretty cold,'' he finished, "but I finally got a lead. Aino's son, Leo, lived in the same New Jersey community that Renee did, and he left town about the same time she disappeared. He'd been her teacher and she also sometimes baby-sat for Leo's daughter. I discovered Leo had died since then, but I traced his route up here to Aino's farm, hoping to find some clues. Instead, I wound up taking Aino to the hospital. And that's how I met Rachel. So, you see, I'm not romantically involved with her.''

Sonia was silent for a long moment before saying, "Then you're more of a fool than any Starzov has a right to be.''

Mikel shrugged.

She frowned at him. "Another thing, young man. You lied to me. How dare you?''

"I'm sorry, I shouldn't have. It won't happen again.''

"The only reason I can forgive you is because your untruth led to my coming to Ojibway, here to this house where I'm obviously needed. Not just any therapist could get along with Aino, you know.''

She shot him a warning look. "Mind you, I

won't have you bothering the poor man with your questions.''

"I don't intend to set up an inquisition, I merely want to ask him about Leo's arrival in Ojibway fourteen years ago. How's that going to harm him?''

"I'll think about it. Is there no one else you can ask?''

"I'm staying here until Leo's daughter, Eva, returns from a visit to Finland in a week or so. She might prove to be a gold mine. But I really do need to talk to Aino. He doesn't even know why I'm in Ojibway.''

"Have you told Rachel the reason?'' Sonia asked.

"More or less. I said I was searching for Renee Reynaud, a missing girl. For some reason Rachel thinks I'm a private investigator and I've let her go on believing it. She doesn't need to know I work for the government.''

"Don't try to fiddle with my mind, young man. I know perfectly well you're some kind of special agent.''

He grinned at her. "That's government, isn't it?''

His grandmother studied him for a moment. "Has it ever occurred to you that, though you expect honesty from your friends and relatives, that you, yourself, are rarely completely honest with anyone?''

"It comes with the territory.''

"Mikel, that's no excuse. You are not an agent when you're with friends and family."

"All right, it's gotten to be a habit."

"Habits can be broken. And, while I don't wish you bad luck in finding that poor missing girl, have you considered that lives may be disrupted by the search alone? As for Rachel, make no mistake, she's the girl for you. If you don't seize this chance to be happy, you may never get another. That's all I have to say for the moment."

With a rueful smile, Mikel watched her march from the living room. When his grandmother announced that was all she had to say, he could be certain of hearing variations on the subject for days to come. It was time to absent himself from the scene.

Sonia poked her head back into the room. "I forgot to tell you, Aino would like to see you. He's in the backyard. But no questions! You let him talk."

He found Aino resting on the lounge so he hauled over one of the wooden chairs and joined him.

"Pretty dang hard to get out of one of those contraptions once I get in," Aino told him. "But that grandmother of yours says I have to rest. I guess the camp-out went okay, hey?"

Mikel told him about the various mishaps, earning a chuckle. "I took my handgun along in case of wild animals," he finished, "but Laurie's porcupine was the closest to a critter anyone saw. It upset Rachel when she found out I had the gun. She seems afraid of it.''

Aino gave him a sidelong glance. "She's never liked guns. I keep my rifle and shotgun hid for her sake. What's your opinion of fishing?''

Surprised by the abrupt change of subject, Mikel took a moment to answer. "I've never had the chance to do much fishing,'' he said finally.

"Ever stream fish for trout?''

Mikel shook his head.

"Then you've missed one of man's finest sports. Wish I could take you out myself, but I'm a ways from that yet. Your grandma's seeing to me pretty good for an old gal. I appreciate that. Appreciate you staying around to help out, too. Thought I'd ask Rachel to take you to my secret fishing hole. She's got her own fishing gear—you can use the new rod and reel Eva got me last Christmas. Break it in for me. It's stored in the attic, so you'll have to fetch it.'' He went on to tell Mikel where to find the rod and reel.

As he climbed the steep attic stairs, Mikel realized the old man's offer of his fishing gear and his secret fishing spot was his way of saying thanks. Feeling inexplicably guilty—Aino had no idea what had brought him to the farm—Mikel retrieved the new rod and reel from its cubbyhole near the chimney and brought it down to Aino. By the time Rachel returned home and came to join them, Mikel had learned the basic elements of fly-casting—at least in theory.

He smiled at Rachel, saying, "Aino says you're taking me fishing tomorrow."

She blinked. "I am?"

"It's your turn to be my substitute," Aino told her. "Any news from town?"

"I heard from Amy's mother that our neighbor across the back forty died over at the hospital in Marquette."

"Jack Metsala gave up the ghost, hey? Mean old goat. Always figured I'd outlast him," Aino said.

"How's Laurie doing?" Mikel asked.

"I stopped by to see. Her mother took her to the doctor right away and he didn't think there'd be a problem. Laurie was unhappy about the tetanus booster he gave her, though."

"So she got stuck with something more than porcupine quills," Aino said. "I'd say it'd make her think the next time, but some never do learn." He looked at Rachel. "Tomorrow, now, I want you to take Mikel to my special place and I expect you two to bring back trout for supper."

"Won't I need a fishing license?" Mikel asked.

Aino winked at Rachel. "Got an honest one here, have we, girl?"

After his grandmother's scolding, the word *honest* echoed unpleasantly in Mikel's mind, so much so that he replied, "Just cautious."

Aino chuckled and told him where in town he could obtain a fishing license.

At breakfast the next morning Mikel found himself back in the good graces of Grandma Sonia, now that she knew he and Rachel were going fishing together. She clearly believed the more he saw of Rachel, the more likely he was to become interested in her. If Sonia only knew he was already too damn interested for his own good. Or Rachel's, either.

Once he and Rachel loaded Aino's truck with the fishing gear, Mikel drove, following her directions.

"You really ought to be blindfolded," she said, "so you'll never give away the location."

"It's my job to keep secrets. Aino's fishing hole is safe with me."

"Do you like your job as a private investigator?"

Mikel hesitated. Hedge, or tell her some of the truth? He opted for half and half. "I'm not one. I work for the government."

She stared at him. "The government sent you to search for Renee Reynaud?"

"No. I'm on vacation."

"But…" She broke off, chewing on her lower lip, then suddenly cried, "Turn left here!"

He was barely able to make the turn in time. "Almost missed that one," he said.

"Sorry. I'll stick to navigating instead of talking. It gets kind of complicated these last few miles."

The final trek turned out to be down an old and overgrown logging road, undrivable after the first tenth of a mile. After she told him to hide Aino's truck in a clump of brush, they climbed out, loaded themselves with the fishing paraphernalia and hiked the rest of the way in to the stream, then upstream to a spot where an old cedar hung precariously over the water.

Mikel soon discovered the theory of fly-casting was not the same as the practice of it, but, as he persisted, he caught on and was elated when he caught his first fish.

"Bravo!" Rachel cried. She, he noted, was already two ahead of him. When Rachel caught her limit, she lifted out the sandwiches and soft drinks from the cooler they'd toted in and packed her fish inside. Watching Mikel cast, she again noted his grace of movement. He never seemed to do anything awkwardly. She sighed. He was such a beautiful man.

After a time, he, too, had all the fish allowed and into the cooler they went.

Both dipped their hands into the stream to wash. "Drinkable?" he asked.

She shook her head. "Aino says in the old days you could take a chance on the streams, but it's a risk now." Spreading the blanket she'd brought, Rachel laid out the food.

Sonia's egg salad sandwiches were soon eaten. Mikel dropped his empty soft drink can into the trash bag they'd carried in and stretched out on the blanket, hands behind his head. Rachel finished her drink, disposed of the can and wondered if she dared lay back next to him. Deciding if they kept talking, it'd be safe enough, she did.

Mikel turned to look at her. "Aino says you hate guns. I'm sorry I spooked you at the camp-out, but I didn't realize mine would bother you so much."

After seeing how close his face was to hers, she gazed up at the overhead leaves rather than at him. "Does your job require you to carry a gun?" she asked.

"Most of the time."

So it was no safe, secure government job. But then, how could a man with hunter's eyes sit at a desk? Whatever it was he did, looking for Renee wasn't a part of it. She wanted to ask, right out, who *had* asked him to search for Renee, but she didn't dare. He might tell her what she feared to hear. What if…?

She closed her eyes, blotting out the sunlight sifting through the leaves, but not her memory of the past. Like the nightmare it had been, it snaked into her mind, slithering past the blocks she tried to put up until she felt nothing else but terror.

When she felt hands close around her upper arms she cried out and opened her eyes. The face she saw bending over her was not from the past. Eyes as green as the leaves overhead gazed into hers as Mikel's voice asked, "What's wrong?"

She tried to say "Nothing," but the word stuck in her throat, and when he gathered her into his arms she clung to him, fighting off the shards of fear that still cluttered her mind.

"You're shivering," he said.

"I—I'll be all right," she managed to say. She'd been fine for so many years now, the past successfully locked away. But Mikel's coming had breached the barrier. If only she dared to tell him everything. Then he'd know, though. And so would the person looking for Renee.

"What upset you?" he asked. "The fact I carry a gun as part of my job?"

"Not exactly."

"Want to talk about it? As Sonia used to say when I was a kid, 'Bring your troubles into the sun to banish the darkness.'"

No amount of sunshine could light her past.

"You do realize," he murmured after a few moments, "that if I hold you this way much longer, we'll be involved in more than me comforting you."

Instead of pulling away, she raised her head from his chest to look at him, aware of what might happen, but wanting his kiss more than she worried about what it might lead to.

Mikel, believing he saw his own need reflected in Rachel's eyes, gathered her closer and brushed his lips gently over hers, giving her time to change her mind. When her hands came up to hold him to her, he deepened the kiss, savoring her taste, which enticed and aroused him. If she wanted what he did, what was the harm? And why was he agonizing over it, anyway? She was a woman, he was a man, both of them were free and unencumbered and he'd wanted to make love with her from the first.

Now they would.

He did his best to take his time, even though, as he gradually disposed of her clothes, the feel of her naked skin under his hands tested his resolve to go slow. He tasted her breasts, thrilling to her moans of pleasure. She was so lovely, to his mind as close to perfection as a woman could be. Her eager responses to his every caress drove him up and up. He was unzipping his jeans when, through the haze of passion surrounding him, he thought he heard a faint but desperate yelping.

Pausing, he said hoarsely, "You hear something?"

She opened her eyes and sighed, pushing away from him. "Something's in pain." Reaching for her clothes, she added, "We have to go help whatever it is."

Standing, she turned so her back was to him and began to dress.

Since she was giving him no choice, as he put himself to rights he tried to determine from which direction the sound came. Now that he could concentrate, he thought it might be a dog. He hoped they wouldn't have to put the poor animal out of its misery. He'd left his gun at the cottage, not wanting to risk spooking Rachel again, but even if he had it with him, he could hardly shoot it in front of her.

After checking the compass he'd bought in Ojib-way yesterday, Mikel helped Rachel gather their fishing gear and other equipment, including the cooler. They set off in the direction they both agreed the yelping came from, pushing through brush until they came to trees tall enough to shade the ground and keep the underbrush to a minimum. Following the sound, they threaded between the trees as the yelping grew louder and louder.

"Definitely a dog," he said.

She nodded. "A wolf or coyote wouldn't do more than whimper, if that. Wild animals don't call attention to themselves, even hurt."

They came around the bole of a large maple and Rachel pointed, crying, "There! See?"

Mikel stared at the brown-and-white medium-size dog whose yelps diminished as it became aware of them. "Help's on the way, pal," he called.

A few steps farther and he saw what was wrong. He muttered a curse. "A trap. His paw's caught in a damn trap."

Dropping what he carried, he hurried to the dog, Rachel at his heels.

"It's okay," he murmured to the animal as he brought out his all-purpose utility tool and knelt beside the animal, speaking soothingly. "Rotten people in the world, aren't there, setting traps for the innocent? We'll get you out of this, don't worry.''

Looking up at Rachel, he said, ''I'm going to try to pry the jaw of the trap apart enough with this gadget so that you can pull his paw free. Ready?''

She knelt beside him, fearlessly touching the injured paw while she, too, murmured softly to the dog. ''Poor baby, you know we're trying to help, don't you?'' Mikel jammed the small pry bar between the teeth of the trap next to the paw and exerted all his strength to try to open the jaws more, all the time hoping the tool wouldn't snap. At the same time, Rachel pulled on the dog's leg and let out a whoop of victory when the paw came free. Mikel managed to yank the pry bar out before the jaws snapped completely shut. He folded up the tool and stuck it in a pocket.

''How bad is the paw?'' he asked Rachel, who was examining it.

''I don't think she can walk.''

''She?''

''Yes, didn't you notice?''

He hadn't. ''Okay, I can carry her, but that sticks you with all our stuff.''

''I can manage.''

Taking a look at his compass, Mikel determined the direction back to the stream. ''Once we reach the stream—'' he began.

Rachel cut in. ''No need. I know this area pretty

well. We can cut over to the old logging road from here by going that way.'' She pointed. "It'll be shorter.''

Which it might have been, but the dog was no lightweight, and besides, he was lugging the trap, determined to bury it so deep no one would ever find it. Since Rachel was also being burdened by equipment, it took two rest stops to get to the logging road, then another before they reached the truck.

"Where's the nearest vet?'' Mikel asked once they were underway in the truck.

"None in town, none close. Our best bet is to take her home and treat the paw ourselves. I'll call a vet and ask him what to do.''

At the farm, Mikel lugged the dog onto the back porch where Aino was sitting on the swing.

"Strange kind of fish you brought back,'' Aino said, peering at the dog. "Looks familiar. Yeah, she's old Metsala's. Got her foot caught in a trap, hey? Rusty one, too. Happens sometimes, those trappers forget where they set 'em.''

Rachel came out onto the porch from the house with a pan of water, soap and some cloths. "Sonia's calling the vet,'' she said. "In the meantime we'll clean up the paw.''

"She was Metsala's,'' Aino said. "Won't have a home now. Nobody lives at his place. Probably why she wandered off.''

"The poor thing," Rachel murmured, washing the paw as gently as she could.

"Guess we'll have to keep her, seeing as how she was sent to us," Aino said.

Rachel looked up at him. "Don't you dare name her Metsala!"

"Wouldn't do, being a she. I'll call her Metsa, how's that?"

They treated the paw, according to the instructions Sonia had received from the vet. She finished by telling them, "He said since no broken bones came through the skin, you can wait and bring her in tomorrow."

"Her name's Metsa," Mikel informed his grandmother, "and she's found a new home."

Sonia nodded. "That's good. A farm should have a dog."

Mikel went off to bury the trap, Rachel going with him to show him where Aino wanted it to go. As he dug the hole, Mikel said, "I don't regret our good deed, but Metsa sure didn't pick the best time to start yelping."

"Maybe it's for the best."

He glanced at her. "You don't mean that."

"We have no future," she said.

"But we do have the present. Isn't that enough?"

She stared at him, her eyes troubled, and finally said, "I don't know."

"It's your decision."

"One I don't want to make!" she cried, turning and hurrying away from him.

He watched her go, wondering what would have happened if the dog hadn't been caught in the damn trap, if they'd made love there by the stream. If they had, would he still have this yearning, this damn obsession for her?

Mikel shook his head. Who knew? But he was more than willing to try to find out.

Chapter Nine

The next day Mikel and Rachel drove Metsa the forty miles to the vet's office. After an X ray and an exam, he decided not to cast the paw. "Two of the bones have what we call a greenstick fracture and they'll heal just as well by themselves since she'll be favoring that leg for a while. Try to keep the paw clean until the cuts and abrasions scab over. Lucky she's a young dog because they bounce back fast. Has she had her shots?"

"I don't know," Rachel admitted. "Her former owner is dead, so we can't ask him. But my opinion is that she's never had any."

She gave the vet Jack Metsala's name, and after his receptionist checked the records, he said, "He didn't bring the dog here, at any rate."

So Metsa got the first of her immunization shots then and there.

On the way back, Mikel said, "The other night you said something about showing me the Porcupines."

She glanced at him, unsure if it was wise to venture off into the woods with him again since she didn't seem to be very good at saying no to this particular man. On the other hand, this was tourist season so it wasn't likely they'd be alone.

"Maybe tomorrow, if Aino doesn't have anything planned," she said.

Back at the farm, Mikel went to the cottage while Rachel followed Metsa as the dog limped up onto the back porch.

"The vet asked if we wanted her spayed," she told Aino, who sat on the swing. "He's going on vacation, but he can do it before he leaves."

Aino eyed the dog, who'd curled up on the rug Sonia had found for her. "She's no special breed, her pups would be hard to place. Might as well have him do it."

"I thought I'd show Mikel the Porkies tomorrow," Rachel said, "if you don't have anything planned. He asked about seeing them."

"I'm thinking about taking the boat out if we get a real calm day. Maybe tomorrow'll be it, maybe not. Why don't you and Mikel go this afternoon? It's not that far. Be sure and show him the mine."

As Rachel nodded, she wondered if she was setting herself up. But she really didn't care—and that was the problem. What she wanted was to make love with Mikel. And soon. Wrong or right.

When she left the porch to go to the cottage, Metsa followed her. Mikel was just coming out and the dog limped as fast as she could toward him, while Rachel took her time.

She came up on them, heard him scolding the dog and hid a smile.

"Look, Lady Metsa," he was saying, "you need to be resting that leg, not trailing after me. Furthermore, you belong on this farm. No use getting attached to me, I'm a no-strings man, and that includes dogs. If you have any sense you'll go haunt Aino and leave me alone."

No strings? But then Rachel knew that. Why should it make any difference? She didn't want strings, either. What she did want was Mikel, dangerous or not. Not forever, that was impossible. Their interlude by the stream before Metsa started yelping was etched in her mind, stirring her emotions every time she thought about them lying together on the blanket. Not forever, no, but for the time he'd be here.

"We could run up to the Porkies after lunch if you like," she told him.

He smiled. "Count me in."

Later, as they drove along the highway beside Lake Superior, catching glimpses of the water through the trees, Mikel said, "In a way this country reminds me of upstate New York. Our mountains are higher, though.''

"The Porcupines are the second highest point between the Adirondacks and Pike's Peak.''

"Whoa. Impressive.''

Hearing the amusement in his voice, she gave him a mock frown. "I suppose you have mines, too.''

"You got it.''

"But not copper mines, I'll bet.''

"I'll grant you that. Do you mean to take me down into the depths of a copper mine?''

"And abandon you there? Lucky for you, I can't. They have the mine blocked off after only a few feet in.''

Once they arrived at the parking area and walked to the top of the escarpment, Rachel waited for Mikel's comment as they, with a few others, looked down at Lake of the Clouds nestled into the dense woods thousands of feet below.

"I can see what Aino meant,'' he said finally. "If you had to climb up all this way on foot for the view from here, it'd be all the more spectacular because you made an effort to get here.''

"You're saying we're more likely to appreciate what we have to work to get?''

He grinned at her. "Spot on.'' Lowering his voice, he leaned closer and murmured, "But some things are more difficult than others.''

He was so close she felt his warm breath tickle

her ear. That, combined with what she knew he
meant, made her insides quiver.

On the way back down, they parked near the old
copper mine and ventured inside for a few feet before being stopped by the grate across the opening.
Even this short distance inside the air was much
cooler. Damper, too, as water trickled underfoot
from a spring.

"Ever been kissed in a mine?" Mikel asked.
Without waiting for her answer, he pulled her into
his arms and slanted his mouth over hers, letting
her go only when they heard voices from the outside.

"I get the feeling we're never going to be alone
on this outing," he said.

She'd known that, but at the same time, had per-
versely hoped they'd find some secluded glade no
tourist would ever discover. That obviously wasn't
going to happen.

When they emerged from the darkness of the
mine, as Rachel blinked, trying to adjust to the
bright sunlight, someone called her by name.

"Well, if isn't Rachel Hill. Never know who you
might run into, do you?"

She stared in disbelief at a man she'd hoped
never to see again—Tim Thompson, not as trim and
athletic as he'd looked eight years ago, but still rec-
ognizable.

Before she could manage a greeting, he reached
for her, obviously intending to give her a hug. She

took a step backward and was brought up short when she bumped into Mikel, directly behind her.

Mikel set her aside so he was facing Tim. "It's obvious the lady doesn't care to be touched." His voice, though even and calm, held an undercurrent of warning.

For a moment she thought Tim was going to challenge Mikel's statement, but he evidently thought better of it, nodded at her and strode off.

Mikel didn't say another word even when they reached the car. Though she'd planned a side trip to view a falls, a glance at his brooding expression made her decide going home was a better alternative. What was wrong with the man? She was grateful she hadn't been forced to endure Tim's hug and would have told Mikel so if he wasn't acting so odd. Impossible that he could be—jealous?

Eventually, Mikel asked her some questions about copper mining in the U.P. and she answered, so the ride home wasn't in total silence, but not one word did he say about the encounter.

Later, at the evening meal, as they sat around the table, Aino said, "That TV weatherman says tomorrow's coming up fair and clear, with only a slight breeze. Sounds to me like a good boating day." He looked at Mikel. "You know anything about boats?"

"A fair amount. Why?"

"Got me a boat down at the marina. Thought we'd take her out and I need a backup man. Otherwise I'll never hear the last of it from your grandma.''

"How big a boat?" Sonia asked.

"Twenty-four-foot cabin cruiser. An old one I use for trolling, mostly, but I was thinking we might take a run out to Kaug Isle, just to get away from the farm. I ain't used to being cooped up.''

"Cooped up?" Sonia echoed. "With all your acreage? Nonsense. Not that the boat trip isn't a good idea. I won't ask if you have a galley, because I don't cook on boats. I might be talked into coming up with a picnic lunch, though.''

"Pasties," Rachel said. "I've got some in the freezer, already made.''

Sonia raised her eyebrows. "Pasties?"

"Nothing like 'em," Aino assured her.

"What's on Kaug Isle?" Mikel asked.

"It's pretty much rocks and trees," Rachel told him. "The Native Americans thought of it as a spirit place.''

Aino had a doctor's appointment in two days, Mikel knew. If the doctor said he was doing well, then Grandma Sonia or not, Mikel would feel free to ask Aino the questions he wanted answered. Meanwhile, why not enjoy a boat ride? Though he wouldn't be alone with Rachel, maybe that was just as well, frustrating as he found it.

The next day, Metsa didn't want to be left behind and howled in misery as they drove away. "Dang dog,'' Aino said. ''Already figures she's part of the family.''

At the marina, Aino let Mikel take over the boat, and after waiting until the bridge over the river swung open to let them pass, he steered the boat out into the lake. Aino pointed, showing him where the island lay in Lake Superior's blue waters, which were calm as a millpond today. After a quick survey of the sky, Mikel was satisfied no storm clouds lurked in wait.

Lake Superior was so vast no land could be seen across it, reminding him of the ocean, except the briny scent was missing. Sweet water just didn't smell like saltwater. Gulls dipped and squawked overhead, following them. As he faced into a breeze that carried the faint tinge of pine, Mikel realized he could get used to this way of life real easy. Maybe he did need to take off from work on a regular basis, the way Steve did.

Later, after they'd anchored off Kaug Isle and were sitting around talking, Mikel, bemused by the sun sparkles on the lake and the peacefulness, remembered Aino's words about the dog. He was, he realized, beginning to feel like Metsa, as though he were a part of a family. He loved his grandmother, exasperating as she could be, and he liked Aino. As for Rachel…

He gritted his teeth. What the hell was he getting into here? Up by the mine yesterday, he'd been ready to kill that guy for even thinking about hugging her. Thrusting the memory away, he told himself he wasn't going to let anything spoil today's peace.

"Expect we're boring the kids," Aino said to Sonia. "Couple of old fogies, that's what we are to them."

"If that grandson of mine ever even hints that's what I am, he'll be sorry," she said.

Mikel stood up. "We could swim to the island from here. Rachel and I, anyway—we've got suits on."

Aino winked at Sonia. "Think he wants to get her alone?"

Rachel frowned at him.

"Are you game to swim?" Mikel asked her.

"If you're asking me, am I capable—yes."

"What I'm asking you is to go with me." Mikel held out his hand.

After several moments of hesitation, she placed her hand in his and allowed him to help her from her chair. "Remember that water is forty-five degrees," she said.

"Even so." As he said the words, he had a strange sense he was asking her something far more complex than to swim with him to the island, but he shrugged it away.

The plunge into the water was, to put it mildly, bracing, and he headed for the islet in a fast crawl, Rachel keeping pace with him. They pulled themselves up onto the large rocks along the shore.

Though the sun shone warm, the light breeze now made them shiver.

"There's a rock ledge over there—" Rachel pointed "—that we can climb onto to sun ourselves."

He saw what she meant and nodded. The ledge was part of an outcropping of rock making a wide shelf that was protected from the prevailing wind by the islet's curve.

When they'd climbed up to it and stretched out on their stomachs on the flat rock surface heated by the sun, they soon felt comfortably warm. When Mikel raised his head he could see the boat, but he knew he and Rachel weren't visible to Aino and Sonia. Not that he meant to take advantage of being alone with Rachel. Not here. Frowning, he tried to decide why not here.

"Something the matter?" Rachel asked, and he saw she was looking at him.

"There's something about this place." He left it at that, unsure exactly what he meant.

"There's a legend about a Chippewa maiden who secretly paddled to this islet in her canoe and then scuttled it so she'd be marooned here. Her lover had been killed in a war party against the Sioux and she wanted to join him. So she set out an offering of tobacco on a large rock and asked that she be permitted to die. When the wind blew the tobacco away, she took that as a sign her wish would be granted."

When she paused, he said, ''I presume it was. Most of these sad tales end in death.''

''This one is somewhat different,'' she told him, ''because, in the wind, she heard her lover singing.

'My love does not remember
She comes here to die
She forgets her promise
She forgets our vow
Only if she remembers
Can we be together....'

''Then she recalled how they would paddle together to this island to be alone and how he once had pointed to a young cedar, tall and straight, and said his spirit was a part of that tree. She then told him she would place her spirit in a birch tree to grow beside him so they would always be together. Trusting in what the wind had brought her, she found the cedar, lay down beside it and waited.

''Days later they found her broken canoe on the rocky beach, but though they searched the islet, there was no sign of her, dead or alive, until the old medicine man pointed to a graceful young birch tree growing next to a tall cedar. He told them to search no more, that her spirit lived within the birch tree. It's a beautiful story, isn't it?''

Finding himself strangely moved by what she'd told him, he said, ''The tale fits the island.''

''Some people believe there's one right mate for

each of us,'' she said. "I'm not sure I believe any such thing, but if it were true, then a lot of women seem to find the wrong one instead."

"Do you have anyone particular in mind?" He asked the question lazily, only mildly curious.

"My mother. My father couldn't have been more wrong for her. In fact, I doubt if he could ever be right for any woman."

Recalling that, like his, her parents were dead, a thought struck him. Maybe the fact both of them had been orphaned as children explained why he'd been drawn to Rachel from the beginning. Or at least it might be part of the reason. "You remember your parents that well?" he asked.

"What child doesn't?" Her tone was bitter.

"I don't recall much about mine except they laughed a lot."

They were both silent for a time. "You know quite a bit about the Native Americans who lived in this area," he said finally.

"They still do, though not around Ojibway. In school, I teach my students there were others living here before us who had different customs, but were also very much like us in many ways. To do that I've had to research the Chippewa—who called themselves Ainishinabe. Chippewa and Ojibway were enemies' names for them."

"Everybody has enemies, must be a human trait." He looked at her. "Like making love."

Her fair skin flushed, making him smile. Rachel was like no other woman.

"What do you think would interrupt us this time?" he asked. "A voice on the wind?"

"Saying we'd forgotten something?" she asked.

His smile faded. He *had* forgotten something. He'd forgotten how Yolanda had betrayed him. Deliberately and in cold blood. How was it he'd come to trust Rachel so completely when he'd known her for such a short time? After all, she was connected with Leo Saari, who might be connected with Renee's disappearance. She was part of the case.

"Now you're frowning again," Rachel murmured.

"Tell me about Leo," he said. "Did he ever give you the impression he was interested in young girls?"

Rachel sat up, hugging her knees, and flashed him an indignant look. "As a teacher he was interested in all his students, but if you're asking me if there was anything abnormal in that interest you couldn't be more wrong."

He sat up, too. "I'm trying to find a reason he might have abducted Renee."

"Why would he do that?"

Mikel shrugged. "If I knew, I'd be that much closer to finding out what happened to her."

"What if you never discover the truth?"

"I will eventually. I always do."

Rachel controlled her inward shudder at his

words. She believed them. Mikel was the kind of man who carried things through, whether it was planting trees with a bunch of Girl Scouts—or hunting down a lost girl. Why did he have to be a hunter? Why couldn't he just be the right man for her? Which would never happen. Could never happen.

"You have eyes like a wolf," she muttered.

"I thought theirs were yellow, not green."

"It's the look, not the color, I mean."

"I agree eye color is distinctive," he said. "That's why it's hard to understand why Renee Reynaud wasn't spotted anywhere in the area after she disappeared—very few people have red hair and amber eyes. I don't want to believe she's dead, so the other alternative is that she was whisked out of the city almost immediately."

"You don't believe she's dead?" Rachel echoed.

He shook his head. "I'm acting on a hunch, really. One that brought me here."

He reached over and tugged one of her hands from where it was wrapped around her knees. Holding it in his, he added, "Here, where you are, someone I never expected to meet."

The way he looked at her made her insides melt. If he pulled her into his arms she wouldn't be able to resist him. Instead he rose and helped her to her feet.

"Let's go look for the cedar and the birch," he said.

Rachel had searched the small islet for them before without success. She was about to say so when she had her own hunch. Together, they were meant to find those two trees.

The rocks made the island difficult to walk around on, especially in bare feet. But Mikel, as though following a marked trail, brought them quickly to a tall cedar with a good-size white birch close beside it. "Voilà," he said. "The lovers united."

As she gazed at the two trees, without willing it, Rachel's free hand came to rest over her heart. She turned to look at Mikel and found him staring at her. Without a word, he gathered her to him and kissed her, a different kiss than before, one that seemed to hold a promise. Or was it a vow? Before she lost herself in the kiss, her last thought was that she was developing an overactive imagination.

She couldn't be sure how long their embrace lasted, all she knew was that it ended too soon. He let her go, stepped back and said, "It's time we swam back to the boat."

Which it was. Though still tingling from the kiss, for some reason she did not want to make love on this island, especially not at this spot.

Back at the boat, they toweled and dressed as fast as they could, taking turns below deck. Sonia poured them each a cup of hot cocoa from a thermos, which warmed them quickly.

"Reminds me of coming home from the ice rink

during a New York winter," Mikel said. "You always had cocoa waiting. And molasses cookies."

"No cookies until after the pasties," Sonia told him. "How was the island?"

To Rachel's surprise, he replied, "Spirits live there."

"Of course." Sonia spoke matter-of-factly. "Islands are magical places."

Rachel thought of the cedar and the birch growing beside each other and decided if she had to choose whether or not it was coincidence, she'd choose to believe it wasn't.

They ate the pasties, still warm from the thermal packing, drank more cocoa and made a dent in the cookies.

"Guess I'll keep you around even if you do nag me near to death," Aino told Sonia. "You got a way with molasses, that you have."

When they got back to the farm, Metsa was ecstatic, trying to greet them all at once. "I see I got to teach you some manners," Aino told the dog. "I can tell your last owner didn't bother."

"Poor thing, she must have thought we'd deserted her, too," Sonia said, patting Metsa's head.

"I thought you didn't much care for dogs," Mikel said.

"In the city, no," Sonia told him. "Dogs belong where they have lots of room to run. This is a good place for dogs." She glanced at Aino and said, "I like it here."

He looked at her and Rachel thought she saw something pass between them, but it was gone so fast she wasn't sure. Aino and Sonia? She shook her head. Must have been that overactive imagination she'd acquired of late.

That night she went to bed and, despite her escalating worry about what might happen if she grew any more involved with Mikel, slept well.

Mikel, though, when he fell asleep, had his recurring Yolanda nightmare, only this time the woman in the dream had Rachel's face. When he woke, heart pounding, he flung on some clothes and left the cottage in the chill of early morning to walk off the remnants of the dream.

Almost immediately, Metsa, who slept on a rug on the back porch, caught up with him and couldn't be persuaded not to follow. In deference to her injured paw, he sat on Aino's lounge chair in the backyard.

"What do you think?" he asked the dog, who was at his feet. "I don't take much stock in dreams. Maybe they mean something, maybe not."

Metsa moved closer, until she was actually sitting *on* his feet.

"Trying to console me, are you?" he asked. "That's not really what I need."

He knew damn well what he needed. To hell with dreams. He needed to get Rachel out of his head. By making love to her? Might be one way to start.

Never in his life, since Yolanda, had he ever stuck with one woman for very long.

Metsa licked his hand.

"Much as I like you, that goes for you, too," he told her.

Chapter Ten

At breakfast, Rachel asked Aino if he wanted her along for the visit to his doctor.

"Sonia's all I need," he told her. "She can tell Doc how I'm doing with the PT—that's what it's called, or so I hear from my expert." He grinned at Sonia.

"You don't mind?" Rachel asked Sonia.

"I wouldn't trust this pigheaded man to go without me. He'd probably try to convince the doctor he could dance on the rooftop."

"Now, that's a dang fool thing for you to say," Aino protested. "What man in his right mind would want to dance on a roof?"

"You know very well what I mean," she

snapped. "You're always trying to push the envelope, like they say today."

He raised his eyebrows. "Listen to her. Sounds like a dang TV commercial."

Mikel got up and poured himself another cup of coffee. He'd been about to offer to go with them to help Aino if he needed it, but decided after listening to the two of them he'd best keep his mouth shut. Aino got up and down the porch steps by himself, so he could certainly get from the car into the doctor's office.

As if divining his thoughts, Aino looked at him and said, "You can give Rachel a hand with the chores while we're gone. Might have lunch in town, too, Sonia and me. Give the cook a day off."

Mikel had offered to help Rachel a time or two, only to be turned down flat. He glanced at her and said, "I'll be happy to, if she'll have me."

Aino frowned at Rachel, who said, "He's a guest, after all."

"Never turn down any offer of help," Aino advised. "Not on a farm. As if we don't have enough work, you know what Sonia wants me to do now? Raise chickens."

"Well, you do have the coop already," Sonia pointed out.

They were still arguing when they left for the doctor's.

Michael helped Rachel with the breakfast dishes.

When they finished he said, "Here I am, ready, willing and able."

She shot him a sly look. "Well, I haven't milked the cow yet. After that, she needs to be turned out into the field to graze."

"Piece of cake. Lead me to her."

"You think so, city boy?" she taunted. "Daisy might just show you otherwise."

"Metsa likes me, you think Daisy won't, too?"

"Liking and milking are two very different things, just the way a dog and a cow are. As you'll see soon enough. Another thing. I wear coveralls over my clothes for milking and general barn cleaning. It tends to keep the smells where they belong. I can lend you a pair of Aino's."

"Thanks. By all means let's keep the smells where they belong."

Aino, though about as tall as Mikel, was quite a bit heavier. After Mikel donned the coveralls she offered him, he glanced at her and saw her grin.

"Lots of room in here," he said, pulling out the slack to show her. "Care to join me?"

"In your dreams."

When they got to the barn she showed him where the milking pails were kept, introduced him to Daisy and pointed out the milking stool, saying, "She's all yours."

Mikel eyed the brown Guernsey, who stared right back at him. "Yo, Daisy," he said to her softly, "I've seen you watching me from the field, so you know I'm not a stranger. Did anyone ever tell you what pretty brown eyes you have?''

As he moved to her side with the pail, he kept murmuring to her. One of the field-training booklets had advised letting any animal get used to you before approaching and he'd found it worked fairly well except with guard dogs.

Aware that Rachel, while pretending to be sweeping up barn floor debris, was watching him, he sat on the stool, positioned the pail, flexed his hands like a pianist about to play a concerto and leaned toward Daisy, resting his head against her side. He put his hands in position and squeezed the way he'd been taught in field training. Daisy obliged and milk began to thrum down into the pail.

In his unit, all the special agents were taught this skill. In a stakeout in the country, you never knew when you might need to milk a cow for food to survive on—or so the manual said. He, personally, had never had to do it, but now the technique was coming in handy.

When he finished, after remembering to do the final stripping, Rachel showed him where the refrigerated cooler was and then he led Daisy from her stall. When he opened the barn door to drive her into the field, Metsa was waiting on the other side and greeted him as if he'd been gone a year, following cow and man into the field. Rachel remained in the barn, and when he returned with

Metsa at his heels, she said, "Okay, I'm suitably impressed."

"I hope so," he told her, grinning.

"I heard you flattering Daisy, telling her what pretty eyes she had. No wonder she took to you."

"If that's all I need to do, I'm willing to say any number of things about your beautiful brown eyes."

"I'm harder to impress than Daisy."

It was warm in the barn and the sun slanting through the open door turned the dust motes stirred up by her sweeping to gold as they danced in the air. Metsa sat down on Mikel's feet as though to make sure he wouldn't go anyplace without notice.

"I really do think she wants to be your dog," Rachel said.

"Wanting and achieving are two separate things." He bent down to ruffle the dog's ears. "You're a good girl," he told her, "and my friend. But when I leave the farm for good, you can't come with me."

"I'll show you where to stow the coverall here in the barn," Rachel said.

"Just in case I plan to make milking a daily chore?"

"Twice-a-day chore," she corrected him.

After he hung up the coverall in what must have once been a tack room, he washed his hands in the utility sink, realizing he hadn't had so much fun in a long, long time. Not that he ever meant to let it leak out that he found farm chores fun.

"Since I've been officially delegated to you this morning, I await my next assignment," he said to Rachel.

She shook her head. "You keep amazing me. Right now I'm standing here wondering if there's anything you can't do or haven't done."

"Before I came here I'd never planted a tree," he pointed out.

"But now you have. Doesn't count."

He nodded. "Let's see. Brain surgery—wouldn't tackle that."

"Yes, but you're not a doctor, so it doesn't count, either."

"You're including only everyday things?"

"Right."

He thought for a moment and then rested his hands lightly on her shoulders. Gazing into her eyes, he murmured, "This isn't an everyday thing by any means, but I haven't yet managed to find the chance to make love to the most beautiful woman I've ever met."

Rachel, transfixed by the intensity she saw in his eyes, whispered, "Maybe you ought to try again." She knew she shouldn't say it, knew safety lay in retreating, but if she didn't take what she wanted now, she might never have another chance. Once he found out the truth about her past, and she feared he would eventually because, as a hunter, Mikel was relentless, that would be the end of anything between them.

"Where?" he asked, the word hanging between them like the dust motes.

She glanced upward and his gaze followed hers. "The hayloft?" At her nod, he took her hand and led her toward the ladder leading upward.

As they climbed, Metsa, left behind, whined and tried to scramble after them but couldn't manage the steep ladder.

"I feel like a kid up here," he told her when they both reached the top. "In the old days, somewhere in the libido of every boy there used to lurk the fantasy of making love to a girl in a hayloft. Today, haylofts are an exotic location, beyond the realm of most kids. In fact, I've never been in one before. And certainly not one in a black barn."

Rachel knew her laugh was nervous. *She* was nervous. Haylofts were familiar enough, but not making love in one. "When Aino makes up his mind to do something, he can't be swerved off course." Staring at Mikel, she added, "A lot like you, really."

"You think so?" Tugging at her hand, he pulled her down until she sat next to him in the hay.

"You are like that and you know it," she said, pausing. "I'll tell you a secret about your eyes. They fascinate me. Sometimes, when you look at me...." Her words trailed off. There was no way to explain how he made her feel.

He took one of her hands in his and ran his forefinger along her little finger, down into the web and up the next finger, his touch a caress. When he finished at the thumb, he brought her palm to his lips. The feel of his warm tongue on her palm sent tingles along her spine. No one had ever before done such a thing—she would never have imagined it could be so erotic.

"You have such lovely fair skin," he said, letting go of her hand to brush her cheek with his fingers, holding her gaze. "If we were alone on Kaug Isle, naked, lying in the sun, I'd be rubbing your bare back with sun block lotion from your neck to your sexy bottom, then down each leg to your feet."

She swallowed, mesmerized, the image of him stroking lotion onto her bare skin pooling heat inside her.

"And then you'd turn over," he murmured. As he spoke, he lifted her T-shirt up over her head and off. "I'd begin with your shoulders." He reached down to the fastenings on her front-closure bra and unhooked it. As he cast the bra aside, she heard him draw in a ragged breath. "Shoulders," he repeated, his voice noticeably huskier. He raised his hands to her shoulders, then slid them down to caress her breasts.

She moaned, swaying toward him. He let her go long enough to yank off his own shirt and then pulled her to him, her bare breasts against his naked chest firing her need, making her regret they were both still half dressed. He found her lips with his in a kiss that told of his own need. He tasted of himself, unique and tantalizing. He tasted of danger and of passion.

Holding him to her, her hands spread across his back, the awareness of the solid muscles under his smooth skin made her remember just what a strong and beautiful man he was. He wanted her, she knew, but no more than she wanted him. There was no one like Mikel. There never would be.

Before easing her down into the hay, he reached for their shirts and slid them under her back. He kissed her again, long and deep, before trailing kisses along her throat and down to her breasts, then lower, lower, rendering her helpless with pleasure. He unzipped her jeans, pushing them down, along with her panties, until his tongue reached her center, sending her into a frenzy of desire.

"Mikel," she moaned.

Then her jeans were off, taking her sandals with them. Mikel murmured, "Open your eyes." When she did, she saw he was as naked as she.

His green gaze held hers as he rose above her. She opened to him, wanting everything, any vestige of fear burned away in the heat of passion. At this moment, he was hers.

His eyes darkened and closed as he slid inside her, murmuring words she didn't understand. Russian? She shut her own eyes, overwhelmed by the surge of indescribable sensations drowning her, carrying her on a wave of wonder to an unknown destination. As in a dream, she heard Mikel groan and knew the wave had caught him, too. They were together.

Some time later, held in his arms, she felt the prickle of the hay under her bare bottom and remembered where they were. "It tickles," she murmured.

Obviously understanding exactly what she meant, he said, "We'll bring a blanket next time."

Next time. The words might have warmed her if she could have made herself believe there'd be a next time for them.

Evidently hearing their voices, Metsa started barking below. Rachel sat up and began gathering her scattered clothes.

Mikel sighed. "I can't say I'm sorry we rescued her, but this is one time we don't need her everlasting devotion." He reached for her, stopping her from dressing, and kissed her. Holding her close, he whispered in her ear, "I don't have any words."

Neither did she, even though *I love you* floated in her mind. Was it the truth? How could she, who had never before really been in love, be sure? In any case, it made no difference, since however he felt about her would soon change, she was certain.

When at last he let her go she felt chilled, even though the loft, with the sun beating down on the barn roof, was very warm. She dressed as quickly as she could. If only she dare tell him the truth, straight out. She was a grown woman now, not a child, why should she be so terrified of a threat from the past? Somewhere inside her, though, that fearful child, hidden for all these years, still lived, as afraid as she'd been on that dreadful night.

With every garment she put on, Mikel felt Rachel draw farther away from him. Still shaken by his own emotions, he couldn't think how to bring back their closeness. What had happened between them left him confused. In making love with her, another dimension had somehow been added so that the very real passion of their coming together was somehow enhanced by—what? He couldn't put a name to it, but it scared the hell out of him.

Picking straw from strategic places, he donned his clothes. The only thing he was completely sure of was that he was going to have the devil of a time forgetting this day.

When they'd both climbed down the ladder to be greeted by an enthusiastic Metsa, Mikel decided he needed to be by himself for a while. Because he knew if he took a walk around the farm the dog would limp after him and she needed to rest that sore paw, he said, "I'm going into town."

Rachel nodded, leaving the barn without a word.

He drove to the park along the beach and stopped there. After taking off his shoes and socks in the car, he walked across the sand to the water's edge, standing there and gazing toward the horizon. Though the day was still fair, the wind had picked up, ruffling the lake into white-capped waves. He began to stroll along the wet sand, annoying long-legged birds into fast-paced running to avoid him. Sandpipers, he thought they were called. Other than the birds, he was alone on the beach.

What the hell have you done now, Starzov? he asked himself.

Exactly what he'd promised himself he'd never do again. Never mind that this wasn't an agency case, the rules were the same. Don't get involved with any of the people directly concerned or any on the periphery, either. You never know.

Because he felt safe in this small town and because he was intent on his own thoughts, he broke another rule—always know what's going on around you. He paid little heed to his surroundings.

"Hi there, Mikel."

The sound of his name jerked him to attention. Seated on a bench near the sidewalk, with a toddler playing in the sand at her feet, was a woman he recognized. He searched for her identity, found it along with her name. Dottie, the waitress from Sylvia's.

"Come and sit a minute," she invited.

With no reason to refuse, he did as she asked. He might pick up some fragment of information.

"Yours?" he said, glancing at the little girl.

"Granddaughter."

He nodded, noticing her eyes, a pale blue, were badly bloodshot. Was his memory failing? It seemed to him he recalled Dottie's eyes being a rather spectacular aquamarine, not this faded blue.

She smiled wryly. "I know I look like Hangover Hannah and then some. All my life I had to wear glasses and I hated them, so I finally got me a pair of contacts, a real pretty color, too. Only I did something wrong and now I've got an eye infection." Reaching in her bag, she pulled out a pair of dark glasses and donned them. "Trouble is, these ain't prescription and I see better without 'em."

"Contacts can take some getting used to." Rachel, he remembered, wore them.

"Yeah, that's what everyone tells me. I hear your grandma's staying out at Aino's with you. Seen her around town in her red car."

"She's his physical therapist." Which was true enough and avoided any other explanation.

"So I guess you'll both be staying for a while, then."

Before he came up with a reply, her granddaughter poured a pail of sand onto his feet. He glanced down and found her smiling at him. "Hi, man," she said.

Dottie shook her head. "Only two and already a flirt."

"What's your name?" he asked the child.

"Mimi."

"Hi, Mimi," he said. She giggled, got to her feet and leaned against his knee, staring up at him.

A horn tooted.

"Oh, there's my daughter," Dottie said. "Pick up your pail and shovel, Mimi, your mama's waiting for us."

Mimi scowled. "No."

Dottie rose and picked up the toys, then reached for the child's hand. Mimi pulled away from her, saying, "No."

"I give piggyback rides," Mikel told her.

Mimi regarded him for a moment, then reached her arms to be picked up. He lifted her onto the bench, then stooped so she could climb onto his back. Gripping her legs securely, he jogged with her over to the stopped car where Dottie lifted her off and into a car seat.

"You must have a kid of your own, the way you handled that," Mimi's mother said from the driver's seat.

Mikel shook his head. "Friends of mine have a two-year-old."

"Well, you'll sure make a great father some day," Dottie told him as she got in the car. "Nice talking to you."

As he walked back to the water's edge, Mikel shook his head. For a guy who'd never had much to do with them, ever since he arrived in the U.P. he seemed to be knee-deep in kids. Just because he'd rather enjoyed it didn't mean he planned to have any of his own. Kids meant marriage and that was definitely not on his agenda.

What was? Finding red-haired, tawny-eyed

Renee Reynaud and getting back to reality. His reality. This area was something outside his experience, which must be why it sometimes felt he was living in a dream world. Or was it because of Rachel?

Beautiful Rachel, with her dark hair and her soft brown eyes. Rachel, who fit in his arms like no other woman ever had. Or ever would? Damn, where had that thought come from?

He couldn't deny he'd never felt so attracted to a woman—which was probably why he'd come close to attacking that jerk at the mine. The thought of any other man touching her... Mikel took a deep breath and let it out slowly. He really did need to get away from this place.

Soon, he told himself. Eva Saari was due home anytime now. With luck she'd provide some closure. Either he was right about his hunch that Leo Saari was connected in some way to Renee, or he was wrong. He still intended to ask Aino a few questions about his son, but he had more hope that Eva was the key. Once he talked to her, he'd know, one way or the other.

About Renee, anyway. But there was nobody he could talk to about Rachel. Definitely not Grandma Sonia, who, misled into thinking Rachel was his girl, had been prejudiced in Rachel's favor before she'd even met her.

He saw the pier ahead of him and turned to go back. Which was easy enough. Except not always in life. Who was it said you never could go back, that once you'd taken certain steps in one direction your course would never lead backward, no matter how hard you tried to retrace your steps?

Grandma Sonia would say he was indulging the dark side of his heritage with such gloomy thoughts. Maybe so, but that didn't mean they weren't true.

Back at the farm, Rachel sat on the swing with Metsa curled on the floor atop the rug. "No strings," she murmured, causing the dog to open her eyes. She smiled wryly, "You've heard those words before, haven't you?"

She had no doubt Mikel meant them—both for the dog and for her. When he said his final good-bye, he'd leave as he'd arrived—with no extra baggage. No dog. No Rachel. This despite the interlude in the loft. Rachel set the swing into gentle motion as she closed her eyes and relived those moments.

Afterward he'd said he had no words, and yet he'd murmured something to her as they made love—words she didn't understand, but he must have. What had he told her with those strange words? If she asked him, would he tell her? Rachel sighed.

Instead of dwelling on what had happened and what she wished might happen, she'd do better to try to wipe all that from her mind, since nothing would come of it, not with no-strings Mikel.

She wondered where he was right now and what

he was thinking. Did he have any regrets about
what had happened between them? Probably not,
men seldom did. Mikel, though, wasn't just any
man. For a few moments, anyway, he'd been *her*
man, whether he believed it or not.

Chapter Eleven

The next morning Aino was in good spirits. After breakfast, he insisted on accompanying Mikel to the barn while he milked Daisy. "Pretty handy fella to have around" was his comment after Mikel turned the cow into the field. "Must get it from Sonia. Sometimes wonder if there's anything that woman doesn't know. If there is, I'll bet she thinks she does."

"My grandmother is awesome," Mikel agreed.

"As long as you're with me, she ain't likely to yell at me for taking a stroll around my own property. Hell, I know I got to be careful these days. Getting better, though. Even Doc said so."

"Glad to hear it." Aino's gait had certainly improved. Making up his mind, Mikel waited until they'd walked awhile before asking, "Would it bother you if I asked a few questions about your son Leo?"

Aino glanced at him. "Why should it? What do you want to know?"

"Why did he come back to Ojibway from New Jersey?"

"Mostly 'cause his wife Betty—she had leukemia, you know—wanted to die among family and friends. She barely made it back here before she did pass on."

"Who was with him when he arrived besides his wife?"

Aino shot him sharp look. "Funny kind of question."

Mikel said nothing, waiting.

"Eva, of course," Aino said at last. "She was only a little thing then."

"No one else? No nurse for Betty?"

Aino shook his head. "Leo took care of her till they got here, then her folks did. Hard on them, seeing her that way. Both of them died not long after she did. You need to know all this for some reason?"

Metsa, who'd been limping along after them, chose this moment to take off after a chipmunk, almost tripping Aino and knocking the cane from his hand. Mikel steadied him, picked up the cane and returned it to him.

"Dang dog. As ornery as her former owner," Aino grumbled. "You never knew old Metsala, but he was a real hammer-head. Your grandma calls *me* stubborn—she should have known him."

Mikel, glad Aino had gotten distracted from the question he'd asked, said, "I take it you still have relatives in Finland since your granddaughter is visiting there."

"Yeah, mostly distant cousins and the like. Most of the old folks Mary and I met when we went over years ago are gone now. "

"Distant cousins like Rachel," Mikel said.

"More or less. Which reminds me. That rod and reel you took fishing when you went with Rachel— I saw it in the back room. If you don't think you'll be using it for a while, you might want to put it where it was in the attic."

"I'll get on it," Mikel assured him.

"Mary got me in the habit of putting things where they belong. Sonia's that way, too." Aino smiled wryly. "Otherwise she ain't a thing like Mary. Got a real temper, she has."

After seeing Aino safely onto the back porch swing, Mikel entered the kitchen, trailed by Metsa, who'd rejoined them after her unsuccessful chipmunk chase.

Neither Rachel nor Sonia were anywhere in sight. Retrieving the fishing gear from the back room, Mikel made for the attic, resigned to having Metsa follow. She trailed him up to the second floor, but hesitated at the bottom of the steep attic stairs. By the time he reached the top of them, though, he heard the dog scrabbling along behind him.

Threading his way among the trunks, stored furnishings and boxes piled on everything, Mikel had just placed the rod and reel back in its niche when a crash made him turn. Metsa stood beside an overturned wooden box he remembered as being on top of one of the trunks. She sat down among the scattered contents as he approached, thumping her tail on the floor and watching him, her expression clearly penitent.

"Okay, I forgive you," he told her. "If you hadn't been lame you wouldn't have been clumsy enough to bump against the trunk and knock the box off. Since it's not your fault you're lame, you couldn't help what happened."

He knelt, fending off Metsa's enthusiastic affection, righted the box and began picking up the stuff. As he lifted the end of a scarf, it unrolled and metal clunked on the wooden floor. Mikel stared for a long moment at the old Colt .45 before using the scarf to lift it by the barrel. He rose and examined his find, jolted when he saw the elk embossed on the grip. The missing Reynaud gun?

Chances of this being a duplicate of Renee's father's Colt were so slim as to be all but nonexistent. What he held in his hand was proof his hunch had been a solid one. He nodded, checked the revolver to make sure it wasn't loaded, then rewrapped the scarf around the gun and replaced it in the box along with the other contents before returning the box to its place on top of the trunk.

Either Aino or Rachel or both had been less than truthful with him. Unless the box had belonged to Leo and been stored up here after his death with no one going through the contents. Possible—but he didn't believe it. In his book, the Colt in the Saari attic had been brought here by Leo from New Jersey. The only way he could have gotten this particular gun was from some contact with Renee Reynaud and Mikel hardly thought it was through her baby-sitting Eva.

He felt certain Leo must have known what happened to Renee, but Leo was dead. Where was Renee now? Who else knew where she was? Aino and Rachel both had questions to answer. And Eva—the one person still alive who'd been in New Jersey at the fateful time and had driven with her father to the Upper Peninsula. Yes, Eva. Instead of springing the gun on Aino and Rachel now, it might be best to wait until Eva got here. Get the three of them together first.

Someone—it sounded like Rachel's voice—called Metsa. The dog skirted him and scrambled down the attic stairs. Mikel followed more slowly, his heart heavy. Much as he didn't want to think Rachel might have lied to him, how could he now be sure she hadn't? It was clearly time to check in with Ed at the agency again. By the time he reached the first floor, neither Rachel nor Metsa was anywhere in sight. When he went outside he saw her car was gone. Admitting to himself he was glad he didn't have to face her for the time being, he got into his car and drove to town. He parked by Sylvia's, near a pay phone, only to have a man stop to use it before he got there.

Cursing under this breath, he waited. And waited. Finally he decided his choice was to get in the car and drive to another pay phone or duck into Sylvia's for a cinnamon roll and coffee. As he hesitated, Louie, one of the townspeople he'd met, walked up and greeted him.

"Going into Sylvia's?" Louie asked. "Me, too."

Mikel found himself nodding. Just being polite, he decided, avoiding the knowledge he was delaying the possibility of having his suspicions about Rachel confirmed by Ed at the agency.

Seated, with his coffee and roll, he found himself wishing he'd gone ahead and gotten the phone call over with, instead.

"Hear you took Aino's boat out the other day," Louie said.

"Aino's not quite ready to handle her yet," Mikel said. "We went to Kaug Isle."

"That's a kind of spooky place. Don't care for it myself. How's the old guy doing?"

"Coming along, his doctor says."

"How about you?"

"Me?"

Louie winked. "With Rachel, I mean. No guy I ever knew got very far with her."

Mikel tamped down his annoyance with difficulty. "We're just friends." He finished his roll as quickly as he could and left the restaurant while Louie was still occupied with what he'd ordered. Seeing the pay phone free, Mikel ducked in and called the agency.

After he was connected with his contact there, he'd no sooner identified himself than Ed broke in to say, "If it's about Rachel Hill, I had to drop that for now. We've got a heavy drug deal going down south we're all tied up with. No time for any side stuff. Get to it when I can."

Mikel hung up, wishing he was back on duty, on an agency case that had nothing to do with the Saaris or the missing Reynaud girl. But, damn it, he was still on vacation and he'd see this one through. Couldn't live with himself if he didn't. The problem was he was beginning to wonder how he meant to live with himself if he did.

As he turned away from the phone, he almost tripped over a little red-haired girl. "Sorry," he told her mother. Then, noticing the child's trembling lip, he crouched down and said, "I better look where I'm going, right?"

She blinked, staring at him.

"Want to shake hands?" he asked.

She shook her head, retreating against her mother.

"That's okay. Maybe next time. Bye." He rose, satisfied that she'd forgotten about crying. Cute little thing, her red hair reminded him of Steve and Victoria's Heidi.

In turn, that reminded him that Steve had told him he was sending some photos to general delivery at the Ojibway post office. He'd forgotten all about it. After picking up Steve's letter, Mikel headed back to the farm. When he pulled into the driveway, he noticed Rachel's car was still gone. He parked and went into the farmhouse where he found his grandmother in the kitchen making an apple pie. His instinct, carried over from childhood, was to seek her out, even though he no longer shared his problems with her.

"The coffee's hot," she told him as she unfolded the top crust over the apples.

He poured himself a mug of coffee, sat down at the table and slit the envelope he carried open. The slip of paper inside asked how things were going, in Steve's unmistakable scrawl. Two photos were the other contents and he grinned as he saw himself in one, with little Heidi perched on his shoulders, her tiny hands clutching his head. The other was a closeup shot of Victoria and Heidi, both smiling.

After putting the pie now in the oven, Sonia came by and peered over his shoulder. "Who is that?" she asked.

"You remember meeting Steve—this is his wife, Victoria, and their little girl, Heidi." He offered her the photo.

"Wait until I wash my hands." That done, Sonia returned and took both the pictures, chuckling at the one of him and Heidi. She handed it back to him, but kept the other, studying it with a frown.

"What's the matter?" he asked. "If you're trying to match mother and daughter, there's really no resemblance other than the red hair. Don't forget what I told you about how they adopted Heidi."

"I am not yet senile," she snapped. "Of course I remember. It's just that Victoria reminds me of someone and I can't think who."

When at last she returned the photo, he peered at it closely, then shook his head. Victoria was an attractive woman, no doubt about that, but whatever else Sonia believed she saw, he didn't. He stuffed note and photos back in the envelope.

"Victoria is the one with the missing sister you're searching for," Sonia said. "A sister named Renee."

He turned and saw she was by the sink, washing dishes, her back to him.

"Yes, she is," he said. "Why?"

"So quick with the questions you are, special agent. I wanted to be certain I have everyone's name correct." She swung around and looked at him. "Here's a question of my own. Why are you so edgy this morning?"

"Edgy? Whatever gives you that idea?" He would have sworn nothing of his inner turmoil showed on the surface.

"It's hard to fool the one who raised you. Have you quarreled with Rachel?"

He shook his head.

"Less than a quarrel, perhaps," Sonia persisted. "What they used to call a tiff. She's off to the vet's with Metsa for the spaying and will wait until the dog is ready to come home. Which means she won't be back until late this evening, so you have time to cool off and to vow to mend your ways before you see her again in the morning."

He rose, thinking if Rachel had taken the dog earlier, he wouldn't have found the Colt .45 in the attic. "My ways don't need mending," he told Sonia.

"Ha! Perfect, are you? Go look in the mirror, Mikel Starzov. Better yet, look into your soul."

Mikel stomped out, trying not to feel like a chastised small boy. Grandma Sonia had no idea what troubled him, so her words should have no effect. Still, the first thing he did when he reached the cottage was stare at himself in the bathroom mirror.

Hunter's eyes, is that what I have? he asked himself. Rachel thought so. He shrugged. His job was to hunt down those who broke the law. In this case, he hunted for a missing girl, now a woman. Not necessarily because she'd committed a crime. Though there was that gun, after all.

Why hadn't Rachel asked him to ride along with her to the vet's? Feeling guilty because she'd held back information, maybe? He turned away from the mirror, shaking his head. Rachel might not know any more than she'd told him. It was entirely possible she didn't know about the gun. That's what he'd like to believe, anyway, even though his experience argued otherwise. He hadn't forgotten how terrified she was of guns. Why?

Finding the cottage too confining, he took a walk around the farm. All the little apple seedlings looked good, not a droopy one among them. Examining them reminded him of the day he and the Scouts had planted them under Rachel's watchful eye. She'd trusted him not to make a fool of himself—couldn't he trust her a little?

Aino was not using the lounge today, so Mikel finally plopped down on it. He hadn't slept well last night because he'd been plagued by his recurrent Yolanda nightmare. Apparently he hadn't yet worked through what the shrink at headquarters had called the "trauma of betrayal" when he'd gone through the required deprograming after the shootout.

But why was the damn dream haunting him almost every night now?

"Take what happened apart," the doc had advised. "Analyze every action."

Mikel hadn't done that. What the hell, it was over and both he and Steve had survived. So had she, he'd heard. Yolanda might be serving time, but she'd be out someday, since she wasn't one of the principal players. Out and ready to entice some other fool she thought could help her in one way or another. Every word she'd ever said to him had been a lie.

He leaned back and closed his eyes, trying to relax, but he couldn't shift his mind from Yolanda and what she'd done. He gave up and decided to belatedly take the doc's advice. Maybe an analysis now would prevent a nightmare later. He deliberately tried to conjure up her face, but, just when he thought he had it, the eyes turned brown instead of deep blue and the face morphed into Rachel's.

"Go back to when you met her," he muttered, and was more successful with that memory, except for the realization of how cleverly she'd engineered it to seem random.

Led him along like a blind pup on a leash, she had. That's what he'd been—an eager puppy, too blinded by lust to realize he was being led to just where she wanted him. Never again.

But hadn't he made the same mistake yesterday in the hayloft? Mikel opened his eyes and sat straighter. He would have sworn there'd been more than lust involved. And Rachel wasn't sexually experienced, he'd swear to that, too. In fact, he was pretty damn certain he'd been the first man she'd ever made love with, an erotic experience he wasn't sure he could ever wipe from his mind.

So, okay, Rachel was no Yolanda. But that didn't mean she hadn't lied to him. He could trust no one connected with the Saari family now that he'd found the Reynaud Colt .45 in the attic. He was so engrossed in his thoughts that he didn't see anyone approaching until a twig snapped underfoot. Mikel sprang to his feet, his hand automatically reaching for the shoulder holster he wasn't wearing. He stared at Aino, several feet away.

"Startled you, did I?" Aino asked.

"I didn't mean to steal your seat," Mikel said. "The lounge is all yours."

Aino nodded and eased down onto it. "Sit down," he ordered.

Mikel complied.

"I ain't going to ask any questions, mostly 'cause I don't want to hear any lies," Aino told him. "It's Rachel I want to talk about." He gazed at Mikel from narrowed eyes. "Don't you go hurting that gal. Sonia says she has faith you won't, but I don't know you like your grandma does and so I have my doubts. Rachel's been hurt enough in her life, she doesn't need any more—you hear me?"

Taken aback, Mikel nodded.

"Good. See that you take it to heart. You best take heed, too, about what I said at the beginning. Don't go asking me questions about my Rachel."

"Perhaps you'd like me to leave the farm," Mikel said.

"No, no, that won't do any good. It's too late.

I'd rather have you here where I can keep an eye on you.''

What the hell had triggered all this? Mikel wondered. Aino couldn't know he'd found the gun. Was it the questions he'd asked Aino about Leo this morning? Or was it merely a reaction to something Sonia might have said about the relationship between him and Rachel?

''I'll keep what you've said in mind,'' he told Aino.

''Mind? What's that got to do with it? The mind's too cunning for what I'm talking about. It's your heart I said and it's your heart I meant.''

Between his grandmother urging him to search his soul and Aino insisting he think with his heart— what a concept—he felt like an alien who didn't understand the language.

''Please excuse me, sir,'' he said.

''I realize you'll do what you must.'' Aino turned his face away and closed his eyes in an abrupt and effective dismissal.

More disturbed than ever, Mikel left him. When he reached his car, he got in and drove aimlessly down the highway, wanting to escape and yet aware he was going nowhere.

In the town where the vet practiced, Rachel, who'd spent the day wandering around the shops, found a restaurant she liked the looks of and had broiled whitefish for supper. By the time she re-

turned to the vet's, Metsa had recovered enough
from the anesthesia to be taken home.

"Try to keep her quiet overnight," he said.
"There's only a small incision, don't worry about
it unless she starts bleeding—which I don't antici-
pate. She'll be back to her normal self by morning."

Since she wanted to keep an eye on the dog,
Rachel let her curl up on the passenger seat in front
as she began the drive home. After a time, she
asked, "What am I going to do? I spent the entire
day thinking about Mikel. I can't get him out of
my mind and I'm afraid I never will. Yet I know
nothing can come of it."

Metsa opened her eyes and thumped once with
her tail.

Rachel smiled. "The trouble is I don't know if
one thump is yes or no, and, anyway, neither of
them answers my question. When he's around I
can't think at all, much less decide anything. I
thought maybe if I drove alone today I could keep
a clear head and come to some decision. No go.
Should I tell him the truth? Yet how can I?"

Metsa moved enough to lick Rachel's hand.

"Thanks for your sympathy. You really are a
nice dog, but you're enthralled with him, too, aren't
you? Another susceptible female, just like me and
my Girl Scouts. My life was so simple until he
came into it."

Routine might be a better word for her life, Rachel thought. Maybe even in a rut. She didn't, she couldn't regret knowing Mikel, but he'd certainly complicated her life almost past bearing. What was she to do?

When she reached the farm driveway, the long summer evening was darkening into night and she still hadn't reached one single conclusion. The headlights picked Mikel out, in the act of rising from the front steps, and she knew he'd been waiting for her return.

She got out and waited for him to walk over to the car. "I'm glad you're here," she said. "Metsa's pretty groggy yet, she'll need to be carried in."

Without answering, without saying a word, he wrapped his arms around Rachel and kissed her, almost desperately, she thought. As always, his kiss blanked her mind, churning her emotions into a frenzy of need, giving her no space to decide whether or not she wanted to feel this way.

One last fragment of realization flashed into her mind as she gave herself up to the magic of his kiss. She loved him, loved Mikel, the hunter.

Chapter Twelve

Shocked by the realization of what she actually did feel for Mikel, Rachel came partway out of the daze of passion evoked by his kiss, enough so that she recognized a difference in how he held her. Always before, she'd been aware at some deep level that he was cued by her reactions. Now, even though she'd drawn back slightly, he showed no inclination to let her go, in fact he tightened his grip and his mouth came down hard again on hers.

Ruthless. The word jarred her senses, making her struggle to free herself. "No!" she cried. "Not like that."

For a long moment, she didn't believe he meant to let her go, but then he released her and stepped back. "You didn't take me with you," he muttered hoarsely.

She decided to tell him the truth. "I needed to be alone. You—us..." Her voice trailed off. She began again. "It's all happened so fast, like a Lake Superior storm."

He sighed. "Yes. One we ought to have seen coming."

Metsa whined from inside the car, reminding them of her presence. "We need to get Metsa in before we go on talking," Rachel said.

"Where do you want her? On the back porch where she usually sleeps?"

"For tonight she'd be better off in the back room. That's where she'll be sleeping this winter, anyway. Aino would never force her to sleep outside in the cold—he's softhearted when it comes to animals."

Mikel opened the passenger door and scooped the dog into his arms. Rachel scurried ahead to move Metsa's sleeping rug from the porch to the back room. When he laid the dog on her rug, she tried to get to her feet but subsided with a whine.

"Take it easy, girl," Mikel advised her. "You'll be okay tomorrow."

But when they tried to leave the room, Metsa stumbled to her feet and staggered after them. Mikel rolled his eyes. "I suppose I'll have to take her to the cottage for the night."

"That might be best. She'll be happier with you there."

"Bring the rug," he said, resignation tingeing his words as he picked up the dog again.

Rachel grabbed the rug and water dish and followed him to the cottage. Once inside, they settled the dog on the rug in front of the unlit fireplace. She dropped her head onto her paws, apparently satisfied since they were with her.

"Want some coffee?" Mikel asked.

Rachel nodded, reluctant to leave, even though she felt it might be best if she did. Whatever he might think, she knew there could be no resolution tonight—or any other night. She perched uneasily on a chair, watching him. Soon he'd be gone, out of her life. How could she bear never seeing him again?

"Sonia took a call today from Eva," he said over his shoulder. "From where she's staying in New York. She's starting home."

Since Eva was driving, that meant she'd be here the day after tomorrow or no earlier than midnight tomorrow if she didn't stop to sleep. All too clearly recalling how Eva tended to get her back up if she thought any of her friends and relatives were being hassled, Rachel tried to quash her inner leap of alarm. When Eva got upset, she wasn't careful what came out of her mouth.

I'll have to make sure to have a talk with her before Mikel begins inundating her with questions, Rachel told herself.

"That's good," she said. "Aino really dotes on his granddaughter."

Mikel turned from the coffeemaker and sauntered over to the fireplace. "And on you as well," he said. "I got warned off."

Rachel frowned. She'd gotten the distinct impression Aino as well as Sonia was actively promoting a romance between Mikel and her. "Why would he do that?" She was really asking herself, but she spoke aloud.

"I'm not sure." He looked over her head, rather than at her, which wasn't like him at all.

"You asked him about Leo, didn't you?"

Mikel nodded. "He didn't like my questions. I got the message that he doesn't care much for me now, either."

"He's touchy about Leo," she said carefully.

"So I found out. I offered to leave the farm, but he refused to kick me off his property. Once I talk to Eva, though…"

He didn't finish the sentence, but he didn't have to. Rachel knew he'd leave once he discovered he couldn't learn anything from Eva, either. And he wouldn't if Eva was warned to keep her cool ahead of time. Too bad Rachel had been at the vet's when the call came or she could have talked to Eva before she got here.

"Was Eva surprised to learn your grandmother was staying here?" she asked, determinedly shifting the subject slightly.

"Sonia never lets anyone stay surprised for long. I'd say Eva knows everything there is to know."

Which was entirely correct. And not only about Sonia.

"Coffee's ready." As he spoke, Mikel crossed to what he'd set up as a serving table and then carried two mugs over, handing one to her before he sat down. "Back to our own private Lake Superior storm," he said. "Are you trying to tell me we're shipwrecked?"

His image brought a wry smile to her lips. "That's one way of looking at it."

"Some ships ride out storms."

Not ours, she wanted to say, but couldn't, true as she knew it had to be. Instead of answering, she took a sip of her coffee, a dark fog of sadness settling over her.

"You'll be leaving," she managed to say after a while, completing the sentence he'd begun earlier. "There really isn't anything more to say."

He took a swallow of coffee, set his mug aside and rose, momentarily startling groggy Metsa. He soothed her before coming to stand over Rachel.

"It's easy to tell the dog everything's all right because it's true for her," he said. "I want to say the same thing to you, but I can't."

"Shipwrecked," she reminded him.

"Damn it!" He turned away from her, pacing back and forth.

She watched him, saying nothing, her heart

heavy with the knowledge that all too soon he wouldn't be here for her to watch.

"I want to tell you a story," he said at last, pausing beside her. Hooking the footstool by the other chair, he pulled it over and sat on it, his back to her, leaning against her legs as he had once before. Unable to help touching him, she rested a hand on his shoulder, savoring the intimacy.

How could it feel so right to be sitting here like this with him when things were so wrong between them?

"Once upon a time," he began, "when I was in the middle of an agency case, I met a woman named Yolanda."

Rachel listened, at first with some confusion, wondering why he was telling her about a former affair, then beginning to realize the point of the story when he kept repeating in one way or another how totally he'd believed in this woman.

"I don't discuss agency matters with anyone," he continued, "and I didn't with Yolanda. Not consciously. But she was shrewd enough to pick up a snippet here and a snippet there, enough for her to put together a fairly accurate scenario of how the investigation into the illegal arms shipment was going, and so she was able to set me up. The only thing she didn't count on was my hunches. I don't know where they come from, but I do get them. And I've learned to pay attention. I didn't pick up on her betrayal, just that something wasn't right and

I yelled at my buddy Steve to get the hell out of that warehouse."

When he didn't go on, she asked, "Then what happened?"

"One hell of a shootout. Steve and I survived because he believed in my hunches as much as I did. But I got us into the mess because I believed in Yolanda's honesty, when she'd lied to me from the beginning. She was a small cog in the arms cartel all along and I never caught on until the end that they'd sicced her on me."

Rachel set aside her coffee mug and caressed his shoulder, aware of how hurt and angry he must have been. "What a cruel and terrible thing for her to do," she murmured.

"So now I've come to believe everyone lies to me," Mikel added.

He didn't have to say "even you," because she knew now that he'd told the story to make her aware he couldn't trust her. Didn't trust her. And he was right. Her hand drifted away from his shoulder, came up and clenched her other hand. He believed she'd lied to him, which she had, but, at the same time, she was almost certain he didn't yet know the real truth.

Tell him! an inner voice urged. She took a deep breath, searched for a way to begin and found she couldn't force a single word out.

Mikel rose from the stool, grasped her hand and pulled her to her feet. With his hands on her shoulders, he gazed down at her. "Don't look so stricken," he said. "I did survive."

Before she could decide how to respond, he bent and brushed his lips over hers in the gentlest of kisses. "Tell me our ship is still afloat," he murmured.

Unable to help herself, she lifted her arms to hold him to her. After all, the condemned were allowed one last request. Hers might be silent, but he'd understand what she wanted.

With a groan, Mikel caught her close. Because of the still vivid memory of how she'd backed off earlier from the way he kissed her by the car, he tried his best not to let the desperation driving him affect the way he made love to her. As he'd told Aino, he would never hurt Rachel. Even though the way he felt about her frightened him, he couldn't help wanting her with an aching passion he'd never experienced before.

And wasn't likely to experience again?

Thrusting that thought away, he allowed himself to fall under the spell of holding Rachel in his arms. He'd pinned down her scent—that of the sweet violets they sometimes sold on street corners in New York City, a delicate scent he'd never encountered elsewhere. Tasting her, touching her was an addiction he didn't know how he'd ever be able to break.

But this was no time to think of the future when now might be all they'd ever have. The certainty came from deep within him, from the place where his hunches arose. There was more to it than his leaving after he'd talked to Eva, but, at this moment, he refused to seek further for the reason why.

He deliberately let go of reality until only Rachel and he existed, the two of them, the fire flaring between them. She belonged in his arms, he was meant to hold her and caress her until the flames consumed them. Kiss by kiss they eased across the space separating them from the bed, clothes dropping along the way. When at last they lay flesh to flesh, her sweet moans of pleasure and need so aroused him that he could hardly hold back. Only the overwhelming desire to make it last forever kept him from plunging into her soft heat and driving them both to completion.

He wanted, he needed to savor all of her and he did his best to satisfy that urge, until her whispered "Please—now" drove him over the edge. Deep inside her, he felt her contract around him, heard her cries and joined her in the rapture of release.

Coming down, he couldn't let her go. He held her next to him, a strange sensation pervading him. Rachel was his in a way no other woman had ever been. He couldn't imagine never seeing her again.

They fell asleep in each other's arms.

He woke when she eased away from him, drowsily watching her gather her scattered clothes and don them. He knew it was best she didn't spend the night with him, much as he wanted her to, so made no move to stop her. But, as she opened the door, he said, "Could be it's unsinkable."

She turned to him and smiled before leaving the cottage, yet her smile had been a sad one, as if in denial of his words. He sighed and, since it was barely light, turned over and tried to go back to sleep. When he finally did, he dreamed....

He walked, barefoot, along a beach, sandpipers scattering ahead of him. Ahead of him red-haired children played with pails in the sand. As he neared, they all ran off, one leaving behind a toy gun. A woman knelt by the water line searching the damp sand. Dottie, he thought, and asked her what she was looking for.

"My contacts," she wailed. "I've lost them." When she turned her face up to look at him, he saw she wasn't Dottie, she was Yolanda. No, not Yolanda—Rachel. As he watched, she began to cry and her eyes changed color—aquamarine, to pale blue to brown, to—

Mikel woke abruptly to find Metsa's front paws on the bed, her brown eyes staring at him as she whined. He sat up, blinking and shaking his head. Taking that as a sign he understood, Metsa limped to the cottage door and waited there.

"Want to go out, do you?" he mumbled, getting up and opening the door for her. Yawning, he watched her head out into the cool and cloudy morning, apparently back to normal.

He wished he were. He could still very faintly

smell Rachel's scent mixed in with the rich flavor of lovemaking and it made him long to have her in his arms again. So much for his theory that his obsession with her would lessen once they'd made love. He wanted her more than ever.

As he showered and dressed, he supposed he should be glad the dream hadn't been a Yolanda nightmare, but it had disturbed him all the same. Redheads, toy guns, lost contacts—if the dream was trying to point up something, he could understand the gun and red hair, but not the missing contacts. Rachel wore them, true, but...

Mikel paused in the act of putting on his shoes, suddenly realizing that he didn't actually know whether or not Rachel's eyes were actually brown. As Dottie had reminded him, contacts could change eye color as well as improve vision. He had no reason to believe Rachel wore colored contacts, though. Or did he?

Troubled, he tied his shoes and left the cottage, Metsa joining him before he reached the house. He'd planned to go to Sylvia's for breakfast in order to avoid eating at the same table with Aino, but the dream had changed his mind. He needed to see Rachel this morning.

Aino was not in the kitchen, but Sonia and Rachel were there, deep in conversation. When his grandmother saw him, she broke off whatever she was saying and left the room, leaving Rachel clearly distressed. Why? Mikel took a step toward her, intending to offer comfort. She glanced at him, then backed away, looking even more upset. A moment later she fled, leaving him alone in the kitchen. The cup of coffee he poured failed to make him feel any better.

In her bedroom, Rachel stared at her reflection in the mirror over her dresser and shook her head. No more masquerade. Reaching for the plastic container where she stored her contacts, she eased them out one at a time and slipped them inside. No matter what came of it, Mikel had to know the truth. Because he'd interrupted Sonia before she'd finished talking, Rachel had no idea how his grandmother had ferreted out the secret—but she had.

As Sonia had said, "I know, and soon he will. It cannot be hidden any longer."

The problem was, Rachel still didn't know how to begin. Still, she'd made a start by removing the contacts. Taking a deep breath, she gathered what courage she could muster up and started downstairs.

She hadn't reached the bottom before the front door opened and Eva breezed in. Crying her name, Rachel flew down the rest of the steps and hugged her.

"How did you get here so quick?" she asked when they drew apart.

"I decided you needed me, so I flew. My friend will drive my car back here from New York in a week or so. She has vacation time coming. I got a lift to Ojibway from Ironwood with the newspaper distributor.'' Eva blinked at Rachel. ''You forgot to put in—'' She broke off, staring over Rachel's shoulder.

Rachel turned and saw Mikel standing in the entry hall. She swallowed and forced herself to speak. ''This is Eva,'' she said to him. ''Eva, meet Mikel Starzov.''

Eva scowled at him, barely managing a nod.

''Hello, Eva,'' he said. ''We meet at last.'' Half-smiling, he added, ''As I can see, the pleasure is all mine.''

He hadn't yet looked directly at Rachel. She braced herself, knowing sooner or later he would.

Sonia appeared in the hallway. ''You must be Eva,'' she said, brushing past Mikel. ''I'm Sonia— we spoke on the phone.'' Turning, she said to Mikel, ''You might bring her bags upstairs.''

''Thanks, but I'll do that myself.'' Eva's tone just missed being hostile.

''Whatever,'' Sonia continued, apparently unruffled. ''In any case, I expect you'll want to freshen up before breakfast.''

''I—'' Eva began, stopping when Sonia help up a hand.

''Your grandfather will look forward to having breakfast with you,'' she said firmly. ''I'll expect you downstairs in about fifteen minutes.'' Her determined smile took in both Eva and Rachel before she turned and retraced her steps down the hall, snagging Mikel on the way. He had time for one last look at Rachel, meeting her gaze before Sonia forced him into the kitchen with her.

"Tawny," he muttered, shaken. "Not brown. Her eyes are tawny."

"Well, of course," Sonia said. "For a special agent you took an amazingly long time to understand who she is."

He blinked at her in confusion, still struggling with the truth. "You knew?"

Sonia shrugged. "After I saw that photo you had of her sister, I suspected. When she smiles, there's a definite family resemblance to Victoria. Hair and eyes are easy to alter these days, but bone structure is not."

"Not Rachel," he muttered, still unable to come to terms with the truth. "She's Renee." As he spoke, it hit him. He'd been betrayed. Again.

"I rather think she may prefer to be called Rachel, since the name has been hers so long."

With an impatient gesture, he snapped, "What difference does that make? She's lied to me from the beginning."

"Why do you think?" Sonia asked.

"Who cares? Lies are lies."

"Did you ever come right out and tell her that her sister Victoria wanted to find her?"

He thought back. "No."

"So there's your reason. Something very bad must have driven the child Renee to leave home.

Don't you think you should wait and find out what that was before you condemn her?''

Gripped by the grief and anger of betrayal, he shrugged, conveying his utter disinterest in any possible reason why.

''No person in this world is perfect,'' Sonia said. ''Certainly you're not. Why should you expect perfection in others, then? I tell you she was hurt as a child and carries that pain with her yet. Because of whatever happened in the past, she was afraid to have her identity revealed.''

Mikel remembered Renee's mother telling him of the one phone call home the girl made after she disappeared, her father grabbing the phone away and threatening her. Okay, maybe she'd been afraid of him then, but she was no longer a child. How could Sonia expect him to be able to forgive Rachel for her lies to him?

''If it were possible to shake some sense into you, I'd surely try,'' Sonia told him. ''Have you no heart? No soul? It's too bad that agency you work for didn't include understanding in those courses they taught you.''

Aino walked into the kitchen, looked from one to the other of them and said, ''Whatever she's trying to tell you, my advice is to listen, boy.''

Up to there in unasked-for, unwanted advice, Mikel curbed his tongue, managed a brief nod that took them both in, stomped from the house to his car and took off.

He paid no attention to where he was going, because it didn't matter. Nothing mattered. How could he have been such a fool as to let another woman betray him? This time, despite the fact he was in no danger, the hurt cut deeper, down to the quick. His chest fell heavy, it was hard to breathe.

He pounded the steering with his fist. Damn the woman! What she'd done was unforgivable.

Chapter Thirteen

The cinnamon roll Mikel ate with his coffee at Sylvia's had no taste. Knowing it was his mood, rather than her baking, didn't help.

"Heavens, you look mad enough to spit nails," Dottie told him as she refilled his cup. He noted absently that she wore glasses today. "Something go wrong?"

"No!" he snapped.

She raised her eyebrows and left him alone after that.

When he came out of the café, the clouds covering the sky had begun to spit cold rain, which did nothing to improve his temper. He eyed the pay phone down the street and shook his head. No, it'd be premature to call Steve and Victoria. Confirmation from the guilty party would be his proof; he needed that before letting them know the lost had been found. Which meant he must go back to the farm for a formal confrontation with the entire crew—Aino, Eva and Rachel, who wasn't Rachel at all.

He should be looking forward to it. After all, his case was solved. Why, then, should depression be mixed with his righteous anger?

Back at the farm, he found everyone, including his grandmother, seated in the living room, waiting. He could have cut the hostility with a knife. Standing, he cleared his throat as he eyed them one by one.

"Among other recent revelations," he said, "I know the Reynaud Colt .45 is stored in the attic. Care to tell me how all this came about?"

Aino opened his mouth, but Rachel spoke first. "I want you to know that Leo Saari was not to blame for anything. Leo was a wonderful man who risked his reputation as well as his professional career to rescue me on that horrible night. If he hadn't, I doubt if I'd be alive now."

She paused and he tried not to look directly at her. Gone were the soft brown eyes; somehow her steady tawny gaze disturbed him.

"My father was an abusive alcoholic," Rachel continued. "By his order, my sister and I weren't allowed to be out of the house without my mother with us, except to go to school. I don't know what he thought could happen to us that would be any more awful than the way he terrorized us when he was at home. Fortunately he was gone a lot. When Leo Saari asked me if I could baby-sit his daughter while he took her mother to the clinic for her treatments—'' she glanced at Eva ''—I knew my father would never agree, so I begged my mother to help cover up for me.''

''She told me that,'' Mikel said. ''You used to wait at the corner grocery by your house for Leo to drop Eva off.''

''Yes. It was always during the day, and we used to go up a block and across the street to a park where lots of kids played. Mothers brought toddlers there, too. It was perfectly safe. Leo would come by there and pick Eva up on his way back from the clinic. He was almost never gone more than two hours, and since my father was never home in the afternoons, he didn't have a chance to find out what I was doing.''

''Your mother and sister told me how your father sometimes threatened all of you with the Colt,'' Mikel said.

''We never knew whether it was loaded or not,'' Rachel said in a tight voice. ''Never knew if we were going to live or die.''

Mikel tried to ignore the pang he felt for the terrorized child she must have been. No wonder she hated guns. Scum like Reynaud didn't deserve to live.

"That last day my father didn't come and pick me up as soon as he usually did," Eva continued, glaring at Mikel. "It wasn't his fault. My mother had a reaction to the chemotherapy and that delayed him. I don't see why you're picking on Rachel, anyway. She didn't do anything wrong."

"Please, Eva, I'll handle this," Rachel said in what Mikel recognized as her "teacher" voice. "None of us—Leo, Eva nor I—knew that, as the day darkened, those who frequented the park changed from mothers and children to drug dealers and their customers. When I noticed what I thought of as bad guys wandering into the park I got scared. Much as I wanted to take Eva home with me, I was afraid to, because of my father. Besides, Leo wouldn't know where we were."

"When it got really dark, we hid in the bushes up by the road," Eva explained, making him decide she was the irrepressible type. "I started to cry, but Rachel put her arms around me and told me we'd be okay, that my dad would be along soon. She was so brave. But then—" her voice quavered as though she were reliving her fright "—then it happened."

Rachel picked up the story. "We heard a loud crack—a gunshot we realized later—and then footsteps pounded toward where we were hiding. I panicked, thinking we'd been seen, grabbed Eva's hand and, telling her to run, pulled her with me into the open. To my horror a man called my name and I—I recognized my father's voice." She took a deep breath and let it out. "I kept running but looked back and there he was coming after us."

"I saw him but didn't know who he was," Eva said. "Rachel didn't notice another bad guy running toward us from another direction and I was too scared to tell her. I don't exactly know what happened next."

"My father ran into the other man—that's the first I saw there was another man," Rachel said. "I froze in terror. When they collided my father dropped his gun and it fell right at my feet. That startled me enough so I could move again. All I could think of was that if he didn't have the gun, he couldn't shoot us, so I grabbed it up and ran on with Eva."

"My dad had just pulled up to the curb," Eva said. "We scrambled into the back seat. Rachel burst into tears and I screamed, 'Bad guys are after us!'"

"I'm sure poor Leo didn't know what to do when I begged him not to take me home because my father would kill me," Rachel said. "What he did was drive to his house, where he finally got a more-or-less coherent story from me. I handed him the gun and I remember him sniffing the barrel. Apparently he could tell it had been recently fired because he swung into action."

Eva broke in again. "He knew my mother was

dying, our camper was already packed to leave for Michigan because she wanted to die at home there. So he carried her into a bed in the camper and told Renee and me to get inside, too. He asked her to put me to bed and to keep an eye on my mother. Then he hooked the car to the back of the camper and drove off.''

After a silence, Aino began his part of the story. "Leo called me from the Soo, just after he'd crossed over into the U.P. from Canada, and explained the problem. By then he'd figured out what to do. I had an elderly cousin in Seney and Leo dropped Rachel off there temporarily. He'd already dyed her hair black to hide that noticeable red, and so, when my cousin brought her here to the farm the next day she was a brunette. Leo delayed his arrival until the following day.''

"My brown contacts came later," Rachel added.

"How about the Rachel Hill birth certificate?" Mikel asked, his head reeling from what he'd heard. He didn't doubt it was the truth, not when he'd watched both Rachel and Eva reliving the terror of that fateful night.

"Fourteen years before, my Seney cousin had a granddaughter who'd died giving birth to a baby girl." Aino told him. "The child didn't live more than a month or two, and knowing we'd need some identity for this poor girl Leo had rescued, he brought the baby's birth certificate with him. Her name was Rachel Hill.''

Rachel stood up and faced Mikel defiantly. "So now you can tell my father you've found me. I'm ready to face him."

Mikel gritted his teeth, finally and very belatedly understanding why she'd been afraid to tell him who she really was. "Your father died some years ago," he said gruffly. "Your sister Victoria is the one who wanted me to find you."

She stared at him for a long moment, murmured "Victoria," and burst into tears.

Without thinking, he started toward her, meaning to comfort her, but Eva reached her first. She put her arms around the sobbing Rachel and scowled at Mikel. "Why in heaven's name didn't you tell her that in the first place?" she demanded.

"Eva," Aino said. "He ain't such a bad fella. Misguided, is all."

"Stubborn and closemouthed, too," Sonia added. "Always has been."

Feeling very much like the odd man out and desperately needing to be alone to sort out his thoughts, Mikel turned away from them all and strode from the room. In the cottage, he gathered his belongings and packed the car, with Metsa doing her best to trip him. He paused before sliding into the driver's seat to reach down and rub her behind the ears.

"You're the only one who regrets my leaving," he told her. "I'll miss you, but you can't come along. This farm is the place for you, it's your home. You don't belong with a man who has no real home.'' It was the truth—all his various apartments over the years had never been more than places to sleep in when he wasn't away somewhere on a case.

As he drove away in the rain, he glanced in the rearview mirror at the black barn and sighed. Rachel and his coming together in the loft had been an interlude he'd never forget. While he did need to be alone, at the moment he felt more alone than he ever had in his life.

Once Rachel had shed all the tears accumulated through the years, she let Eva talk her into resting and fell into a deep sleep. When she woke, the dimness beyond her windows told her it was still raining and also that it was getting on for evening. She sat up, feeling drained.

As though she'd been waiting for the slightest sound from Rachel's bedroom, Eva popped through the door. ''How do you feel?'' she asked, sitting on the bed.

''I'm all right.''

''What a cruel man,'' Eva said. ''How did you stand him?''

''Mikel's not cruel.''

Eva snorted in disbelief. ''At least he had the sense to cut and run, I'll grant him that.''

Rachel stared at her. ''Mikel's gone?''

''Bag and baggage. And good riddance.''

He'd left without a word. Left her without even saying goodbye. Rachel sighed. What had she expected?

Eyeing her narrowly, Eva said, "Don't tell me you're sorry."

Rachel tried for a smile. "All right, I won't."

"Good. For a minute there you had me worried you might have fallen for him. I should know you've got better sense than that."

Because Eva was younger than she and also because, being older, she'd had to assume a mothering role, Rachel had never completely confided in her and knew she couldn't now.

"It's more than I can say for grandfather," Eva added. "I can tell he's sliding off the deep end over Sonia. I wonder about that. She's a bit tart-tongued, isn't she?"

Correctly interpreting this, Rachel said, "Scolded you, did she?"

Eva shrugged. "I momentarily forgot she was Mikel's grandmother. She didn't take kindly to my comments about him."

"I don't, either, you know. You're entitled to your opinion, but it's not the same as mine."

"Whoa. Maybe you're not as sensible as I thought. You couldn't have let that rat seduce you!"

Instead of a refutation, Rachel said, "Hunters have their own fascination."

"Hunter. Yes, I'll grant he is that."

"Did you know Mikel saved Aino from a far more serious stroke? He might even have died."

"Grandfather mentioned that." Eva's tone was begrudging.

Rachel slid her legs over the edge of the bed and gave Eva a quick hug before getting up. "I know why you want to blame Mikel. Even as a child you were quick to defend those you thought were helpless as well as those you loved. I hope I qualify as a loved one, but I'm not helpless."

"He got past your defenses, didn't he?"

"What defenses?"

Eva rolled her eyes. "Come on, you've been fending off men for years. I'm not exactly stupid, you know. I understood why."

Refusing to deal with that right now, Rachel looked in the mirror and grimaced. "I look like something even Metsa would refuse to acknowledge as human."

"Where on earth did that dog come from, anyway?"

"You won't like to hear that it was Mikel who rescued her from a trap. Her paw was injured, that's why she limps." Turning to face Eva, she added, "In a strange way, he rescued me, too. I intend to get my hair cut and let it grow out to its natural color. No more hiding."

"I guess I can get used to you with red hair again. Just don't expect me to go back to calling you Renee."

"As Rachel I've had the chance to live and thrive. Poor Renee would never have gotten that chance, so I'll always be Rachel." She sighed. "I can't be sorry my father is dead."

Eva gave an exaggerated shiver. "Me, neither. I sure remember the nightmares I used to have about that awful night."

Later, when they were in the kitchen helping Sonia fix supper, Rachel said to her, "I hope you won't feel you have to leave because Mikel's gone. I don't know what Aino would do without you."

Sonia smiled. "We do get on well, Aino and I. As for Mikel, once he was grown, he went his way and I mine. In his way he loves me, but I know I try his patience sometimes. Partly because I won't let him forget he's not perfect, mind you. Where he works, they call him Nemesis, you know. He didn't tell me, but I have my own secret ways. I heard his friend Steve call him by that name."

"Nemesis?" Eva said.

"Because when he's on a case, he always gets the bad guys," Sonia explained.

"Rachel's certainly no bad guy!"

"Don't forget finding her was his wedding gift to his best friend, Steve, the man who married Renee's sister."

Eva grimaced.

"She doesn't want to be convinced Mikel might be one of the good guys," Rachel told Sonia.

"Will you stop defending him." Eva sputtered.

"If he's so great, how come he took off without a word to any of you?"

Rachel, who was searching her memory for where and when Mikel had used the word, Nemesis, didn't answer and she didn't listen to Sonia's response.

They'd been in the loft and she'd just told Mikel he was someone who couldn't be swerved off-course.

"Nemesis, in fact," he'd said. She hadn't understood the darkness in his voice at the time, but she did now.

He'd kissed her then and the world had gone away. Rachel sighed. Whatever Mikel had been called, now he was gone and reality was back to stay. She tried to find some satisfaction in the knowledge that her long masquerade was over.

Turning to Sonia, Rachel asked, "Mikel will contact my sister, won't he?"

"You can be sure he will."

Rachel tried to imagine what it would be like to be reunited with a sister she hadn't seen in fourteen years. Her guilt at abandoning Victoria had been assuaged by taking care of Eva all these years, but now she wondered if her sister had forgiven her. Her mother, she knew, would have been glad Renee had escaped from the abuse, but she also must have grieved, never knowing what had happened to her other daughter.

Rachel sank down into a chair, laid her arms on

the table and dropped her head onto them. Would her mother and her sister ever be able to forgive her?

After a time she felt a warm hand on her shoulder. "You did what you had to at the time," Sonia said. "No person in this world can do any more than that. I left my family behind in Russia to come to the United States, so I know some of what you must be feeling."

Rachel lifted her head to look at Sonia, who smiled at her. "Also, whether you want to hear this or not, you haven't seen the last of my inconsiderate grandson," Sonia added.

"He's the last one she needs to ever meet up with again," Eva insisted.

"No one knows Rachel's heart except herself," Sonia told her. "Now, I'll leave you girls to finish up here so I can work with Aino on his arm exercises before we eat. His leg is now close to normal functioning, but the arm has a ways to go."

"She's really something," Eva said after Sonia left the kitchen. "A takeover person from the get-go."

"Exactly what your grandfather needed," Rachel reminded her. "I thought at first they didn't care for each other because they're always squabbling, but I finally realized they both enjoy it."

"It's not that I don't like Sonia." Eva sounded defensive. "It's just that I left for Finland with Grandpa Aino in good health and you…" Her words trailed off.

"I'll survive. I always have."

Eva sighed. "I guess I can't wish Mikel had never tracked you down because then you might never have been reunited with your family. I can wish, though, that he'd been less of a hunk."

Her words brought a smile to Rachel's face. "So you noticed that, did you?"

Shrugging, Eva said, "I *am* female, after all, no matter what else I might think of him."

To switch the trend of the conversation to Eva, Rachel said, "Did you meet any Finnish hunks?"

"The one I liked the best was too much the strong, silent type. Like Dad was, only more so. Finns tend to be like that, I guess." She laughed. "I'm certainly atypical, you can't shut me up."

"That's why you're so easy to get along with. I always know how you feel."

"I guess. But I can't say I always know how you feel. Like now. What happened between you and Mikel?"

I fell in love with him, Rachel admitted to herself. "We were attracted to each other," she told Eva.

"Too bad."

Rachel let the word hang between them, knowing she could never explain to Eva—or anyone—just how much Mikel had meant to her.

Mikel's letter arrived the next day, addressed to Sonia. In it was a note with Victoria Henderson's phone number, but no other message for Rachel.

Rachel hadn't really expected one, but it hurt all the same that he hadn't said goodbye, in person or by mail. With a sigh, she did her best to put her regrets behind her as she picked up the slip with the number on it and headed for the phone.

Chapter Fourteen

On his return home, Mikel checked in with the agency and found the drug kingpin down south had been apprehended, which gave Ed time to run down some additional information for him—details of the unsolved homicide that occurred the night Renee disappeared.

Three days later Ed reported that the unofficial consensus from the police force in that New Jersey town had been that the victim had been killed in a confrontation by his partner, a known drug dealer. With the murder gun missing, though, it could never be proved. Renee's father, who had no criminal record, had never been implicated, even as a witness.

Still smarting over the lies Rachel had told him, at first Mikel didn't do anything with this information. When he received a letter from his grandmother a week later, telling him she wasn't sure when she'd be returning to New York, he scanned it for news of Rachel. There was none.

Finally after a few days had gone by, he decided no matter how he felt about her, the decent thing to do was to call Rachel and let her know her father had never been implicated in the shooting that occurred in the park, that the cops figured the dead man had been killed by his drug-dealer partner. It wasn't that he wanted to hear her voice, he was just being courteous.

Aino answered the phone and Mikel tried to ignore his pang of disappointment. "Rachel's not here," Aino said, sounding surprisingly cordial. "She's in Nevada."

Taken aback, Mikel repeated, "Nevada?"

"Yeah. After you sent Victoria's phone number, Rachel called her and then flew down to Virginia. They went together to visit their mother in Florida and now Rachel's gone with her sister to some ranch near Reno where Victoria's husband's sister lives, if I recollect right."

"I'll give you a message for her, then," Mikel said, and told him what he'd found out about Rachel's father. "It set me to wondering if Reynaud might have lent the killer his gun. When he saw the armed killer heading for his daughter, he might well have tried to head him off, they collided, and that's when the gun was dropped. Reynaud could actually have been trying to protect the two girls.''

''Possible, I'd say. I'll let her know. Your grandma's pestering me to give her the phone, so I better.''

''Mikel?'' Grandma Sonia said.

''I can't deny it. How are you getting along?''

''Very well. The Upper Peninsula has proved so beneficial for my allergies I may decide not to return to New York.''

Mikel smiled. *Her allergies.* What she meant was she didn't want to leave Aino.

''I can tell what you're thinking,'' she continued, ''but that's my business. As for you, if you had the sense you were born with, you'd know what to do about yours. Why do you keep telling yourself words are truth or lies when the only real truth lives in the heart?''

After he said goodbye, Mikel wandered to the window of his apartment and stared morosely out at the rain. Why did it seem to rain wherever he went? He still had almost a week of vacation left and there wasn't one damn thing he cared to do with the time. His grandmother's words buzzed in his head like a pesky fly he couldn't swat. What in hell did she expect of him? He was the victim, not the betrayer.

When the phone rang he all but snarled into it.

"What's bugging you, man?" Steve asked from the other end.

"Sorry. Lousy mood, that's all. What's up?"

"You soon will be. I got reservations for you, so get your butt on that plane to Reno. I'll pick you up there. You'll be staying with us at my brother-in-law's ranch. No argument. Here's the schedule." Steve rattled off the airline, flight number and time. "Go pack," he ordered before cutting the connection.

Not until he boarded the jet at Dulles did Mikel realize why he was obeying Steve without question. Since this wasn't an agency case, with Steve the senior special agent, that had nothing to do with it. And he wasn't on this flight as a favor to Steve just because they were good buddies. He was flying to Nevada because that's where Rachel was, and regardless of what had happened, he desperately wanted to see her one last time.

He was lucky enough not to be seated next to anyone who wanted to talk, because he was in no frame of mind for idle conversation. On the other hand, that left him a victim of his own thoughts and he didn't much care for those. Why had he insisted on equating Rachel with Yolanda?

Okay, she'd lied to him. But were her lies intended to harm him the way Yolanda's had been? His failure to suspect that Yolanda might have a tie-in to the illegal arms-shipping syndicate had nearly cost both Steve's life and his. Rachel's lies, though, hadn't been meant to harm, they'd been to protect herself and the Saaris, the people who'd rescued her, who'd sheltered her. Yolanda had truly betrayed him, Rachel had not. Except in his own mind.

By the time the plane set down in Reno, he was ashamed of his behavior. Aino had called him misguided, Grandma Sonia had called him stubborn and closemouthed. They were right on all counts. Now, what the hell was he going to say to Rachel when they came face-to-face? She might refuse to even speak to him, and he could hardly blame her.

Steve hustled him through the airport and out to a red Jaguar. "One of Talal's," he said. "You remember him—my other brother-in-law. We're staying at Zed's."

Mikel nodded, having sorted out Steve's identical twin brothers-in-law, Talal and Zed, at Steve and Victoria's wedding.

Steve maneuvered the car from the parking area and onto the freeway before he said, "Since you're not asking why I shanghaied you out here, you must have some idea."

Being with Steve lifted Mikel's spirits some. "Your wish is my command," he said.

"How about those famous hunches of yours?"

"Left 'em home."

Steve shot him a look. "Come on, man."

"I know why I came," Mikel admitted.

"'Cause you done her wrong, right? Victoria

said you'd figure that out sooner or later. She wasn't willing to wait for later, so here you are in beautiful northern Nevada, with the sun going down behind the Sierras.''

''It was raining when I left Dulles—Reno's an improvement. What's Victoria expect me to do?''

Steve shrugged. ''Who knows? But you're just in time for one of Zed's famous barbecues tomorrow. Anything can happen.''

Mikel looked at him. ''What do you mean?''

''You won't know till it hits you. I sure didn't.''

''Sounds ominous.''

''Nevadans prefer direct action to being subtle.''

Raising an eyebrow, Mikel said, ''You mean I might get hanged for my sins?''

Steve grinned. ''Worse than that—far worse.''

Whatever Steve was referring to didn't bother Mikel. What did worry him was meeting Rachel again. To take his mind off that, he concentrated on the scenery, noticing that only a small patch of snow remained atop Mount Rose. Then they entered the open valley where the calm waters of Washoe Lake caught the last pink glow of the alpine-glow sunset. Northern Nevada always surprised him with its diverse beauty.

''Saying your prayers?'' Steve's voice was amused.

''Trying to decide the best way to eat crow,'' Mikel admitted.

''You can never pretty it up enough so it tastes

like anything else, so you might as well take it straight.''

''Is she all right?''

''If you mean Victoria, she's fine and you're her current hero. Heidi's growing so fast she changes daily. Rachel seems kind of dazed since she got here. No wonder, being confronted with this extended family Victoria and I are tangled up with is enough to confuse anyone. Interesting she decided to stay with the name Rachel rather than going back to Renee.''

''Yeah.'' If he ever talked to anyone about his relationship with Rachel, Steve would be that person, but Mikel couldn't bring himself to discuss any part of it. Instead, he told Steve what Ed had gotten from the New Jersey cops and laid out his theory about Reynaud, ending with, ''I'm not saying he wasn't a bastard, because he was. When push came to shove, though, I have a hunch he tried to protect his daughter.''

''I can see he might have.''

After a time, Mikel said, ''I take it there'll be a mob at the ranch for the barbecue.''

''What else? Almost everyone is a relative in some way or other. You met most of them at our wedding.''

''Don't expect me to sort them all out.''

''Doesn't matter. There are a couple new ones. Doc Walker's sister, Laura, married a guy named Shane Bearclaw. And I know there must be a baby or two more since then. It's Victoria's job to keep track of whose they are and their names—I lose track."

The car nosed over the last hill and the lights of Carson City spread out below them. If Mikel remembered correctly, it was another twenty or so miles to Zed's ranch in Carson Valley. In a half hour, give or take a few minutes, he'd be face-to-face with Rachel. He took a deep breath and let it out slowly. As Sonia had pointed out, truth isn't necessarily in words—yet words were all he had to offer Rachel.

How different she'd looked without those brown contacts. The true color of her eyes was almost golden, beautiful, but different. It would take getting used to.

Not that he'd be around that long. Apology didn't come easy to him, but he'd get it done and get out. Fast.

"With that crowd, nobody'll miss me if I'm not at the barbecue," he told Steve.

Steve glanced at him. "What're you crazy? It's being held in your honor."

Mikel realized he was trapped. "My grandmother should be here in my place," he muttered. "She knew who Rachel was before I did. Caught the resemblance to Victoria in that photo you sent me."

"How is your grandmother?" Steve asked.

"Fighting with a Finn who enjoys the arguing as

much as she does. He's Aino Saari, the father of the man who rescued Renee, accounting for her disappearance.''

''Sounds serious.''

Mikel nodded morosely. He didn't begrudge Aino and Sonia happiness, but he sure as hell was far from happy. Who could be in his shoes? Especially since he'd come to realize no one but himself was responsible for his unenviable position.

''We wanted to bring Victoria and Rachel's mother with us to Nevada,'' Steve said, ''but she's afraid of flying. When Rachel and Victoria went to see her in Florida, their mother said that now all her prayers had been answered, but they both got the impression she seemed relieved when they left.''

''Doesn't want her routine disrupted,'' Mikel said. ''I got that impression when I talked to her before I drove to Michigan.''

After a time Steve said, ''Here we are,'' and turned the car into a winding driveway, pulling up and parking near the ranch house. Mikel collected his bag and followed him to the back door.

''Why is it everyone always comes in through the back door when my kitchen is a mess?'' Steve's sister Karen complained before she hugged Mikel. ''You look in dire need of sustenance,'' she said. ''Ham sandwich? Coffee?''

''Later,'' Steve told her. ''What he needs right now isn't food.''

Karen nodded. "Try the solarium. I think Victoria and Rachel are admiring my lemon tree—it actually has five lemons on it."

Steve led the way. When they reached the addition and stepped into the long room with one outside glass wall, at first Mikel saw only Victoria. Then she moved toward Steve, revealing Rachel, who'd been behind her. For a moment, Mikel forgot to breathe, unable to move or speak. He couldn't look away from her, from those unfamiliar tawny eyes in that face he knew so well.

"Your hair is still black," he said inanely, the first words he could manage to get out.

"Yes, I had it cut, but it'll take time to grow in red again." Rachel wondered at the calmness of her voice when her heart was thudding wildly in her chest. She wanted to look away from his green gaze, but could not.

At last he broke the contact when he glanced around. She did, too, and saw Steve and Victoria had wandered away.

"I should have said hello and how are you," Mikel told her, not moving any closer, for which she was grateful.

She returned his hello and added, "I'm finding Nevada interesting."

"Yes, it is."

Rachel searched for something more to say, uncomfortable with the awkwardness between them. "You've been here before, I understand."

He nodded.

After a silence that went on far too long, Rachel said, "Aino called me. He told me what you'd found out about my father. I want to thank you for making me realize he might not have been the monster I always believed he was. It's lifted a weight from my mind."

"That's good." Mikel cleared his throat. "I shouldn't have accused you of lying, especially since I lied by omission myself. I tend to be secretive, it's a carryover from my job. There was no reason why I shouldn't have told you your sister was the one trying to find you. If I had, none of the misunderstandings would have taken place."

He was actually apologizing! "I could have asked," she admitted, with a tentative smile.

Mikel smiled, too.

They still stood several feet apart and Rachel could feel how taut her muscles were. Part of her wanted to reach out to him, but she did not. Yes, he'd apologized, but he didn't seem like the Mikel she knew. Or thought she knew.

He cleared his throat again. "How long are you staying here?"

"Until my sister leaves. Then I'll be returning to the U.P."

"I remember you were going back to school to get your master's."

"Yes. I may miss some classes, but not too many." How stiff they both sounded. As though they were strangers. Worse, strangers who had nothing in common.

"That door leads outside." Mikel gestured toward the glass wall.

She nodded.

"I don't know about you, but I feel suffocated," he told her.

She knew exactly what he meant. Perhaps it was the dry Nevada air. Or the 4,500-foot elevation. Except she knew it was neither the dryness nor the altitude, since they hadn't bothered her before he arrived.

Ever since Victoria had told her about Steve's call to Mikel, Rachel had been rehearsing what to say to him. None of which she'd actually said other than thanking him for what he'd found out about her father.

She watched Mikel slide open the door, telling herself she wasn't going out there with him, even if he invited her. Which he hadn't. Why should he when he probably wanted to get away from her as much as she hoped he'd leave her alone?

As he started through the door, he turned his head and glanced at her with no particular expression on his face. His eyes, though, those green hunter's eyes, looked lost. Rachel found herself trailing after him into the warm evening, so much darker here at this early hour than in the U.P.

"It's the Sierra effect," he said, as though reading her mind. "No horizon to the west, just mountains."

Rachel spoke without thinking, "That's how I feel—no horizons."

"I know the feeling well," he said.

For a moment they stood looking at each other in the light shining through the glass wall, then Mikel turned away from her. "I'll show you the gazebo," he said.

They walked side by side along the brick path, not touching, but she didn't need to touch him to be acutely aware of the tension accumulating between them. Never had she been so aware of any man.

"Have you gone back to work?" she asked, more to be saying something than out of curiosity.

"Not yet."

"Victoria says Steve's gone a lot. I understand he works for the same agency you do."

"Special agents rarely have regular hours."

Which ended that conversational lead. Rachel saw the gazebo ahead, made of wood, painted white. Under the rising moon it looked incredibly romantic. She stopped abruptly. No way was she in a romantic mood.

Mikel halted. "Something the matter?"

"Why should there be?"

He shrugged.

"I think I'll go back to the house," she said, not moving.

"Probably wise." He didn't move, either, just stood there staring down at her.

"In the moonlight, I can't see the color of your eyes," he murmured. "They could still be brown."

She couldn't see the color of his, either, but the softness in his voice trickled heat along her nerves. "Don't you like their real color?" she asked.

"It's a case of getting used to it. Actually, your eyes are beautiful."

He sounded as though he meant every word and she couldn't help being pleased. She thought about what she'd rehearsed to say to him and tossed it all aside. Instead, on impulse, she said, "There's something I've wanted to ask you. You remember when we were up in the Porcupine Mountains at the old copper mine?"

"Vividly."

"Why did you get so upset at Tim Thompson?"

"Was that the jerk's name? I suppose you wanted to let him hug you."

"No! I was backing away when you stepped between us. I meant to thank you, but afterward you seemed so angry, I never did."

"Jealousy," he muttered.

A stab of pure delight transfixed her. He hadn't wanted another man to touch her. "Oh, Mikel," she whispered.

She couldn't be sure which of them took the first step closer. All she knew was that she was in his arms and on fire from his kiss.

Chapter Fifteen

Rachel snuggled closer to Mikel as he deepened the kiss. All her reservations about him faded and vanished in his arms. There was no promise in his kiss, only passion, as wild and untamable as the fire burning within her.

"I need you," he breathed against her lips.

As she needed him. When he held her like this, nothing else mattered.

She lived for this moment, no other time existed. If only it would never end.

"How can I ever let you go?" he murmured, as if echoing what was in her heart.

In this Western setting, so different from anything she was accustomed to, anything might happen. Even a happily-ever-after ending for her and Mikel? Get real, an inner voice whispered. Wanting only to stay where she was, she tried to ignore the warning and was succeeding when she heard childish voices and a dog's bark.

She pulled away. "That's Danny and Tim," she said breathlessly. He must know Danny was Zed's son and that Tim belonged to Zed and Talal's sister, Jade. "And Danny's new dog."

Mikel let her go. "Might've known there'd be a dog to interrupt," he muttered.

As she smiled, reminded of Metsa, the two boys burst into view, chasing a small black dog. "Don't let him get the ducks," Danny cried.

In the duck pond beyond the gazebo, Rachel knew he meant. Mikel swooped down and caught the dog, cradling him under one arm.

"He doesn't look big enough to do much damage," Mikel told the boys.

"Yeah, but the ducks don't know that," Danny said, reaching up for the furry black dog.

"You're Mikel," the other boy, Tim, said. "I remember you from before."

"Good memory," Mikel told him.

"You're like Steve, you catch bad guys," Tim continued. "That's what I'm gonna do when I grow up."

Danny stared at him. "You told me you were gonna be a doctor like your dad."

"Maybe I'll do both," Tim shot back.

"Ha. You won't have time."

"Will, too." Off they went with the dog, arguing.

Mikel looked at her. "We weren't fishing this time," he said softly, "but I like what I caught."

For Rachel, the mood was broken and she turned away toward the house, not sure she wanted him to think she was "caught," even if she was. "It's time for me to say good-night," she said.

When she was finally in bed, though, she was a long time courting sleep before it came to her.

In the morning, Rachel woke to a tap at her door. Before she could respond, a voice called, "It's Victoria. With coffee and breakfast."

Glancing at the bedside clock, Rachel was surprised to see it was almost nine. She hurried to open the door and Victoria entered with a tray, which proved to be the kind with feet that could be unfolded to set on the bed.

"So prop yourself up against the pillows and enjoy," Victoria said. "Karen makes fabulous cinnamon rolls."

"They smell heavenly," Rachel agreed as she obeyed. "But you shouldn't be waiting on me."

"I'm a nurse, remember? We're tenders of the sick and disabled."

"I'm not—" Rachel began.

"Tell me no lies." Though Victoria's voice was

teasing, Rachel winced inwardly, remembering the lie she'd lived for so many years.

"I'm surprised you can forgive me," she told her sister. "I ran off and abandoned you to that abuse."

Victoria shook her head. "We've been over that and I've already told you that our mother left him less than a year after you disappeared." She set the tray next to Rachel. "Enjoy."

Besides the rolls and coffee, the tray held a small plate of apricots. Taking one, Victoria sat on the bed and took a bite. "Mmm, nothing like fruit right off the tree."

After a half a roll and several swallows of coffee, Rachel continued the sentence her sister had interrupted. "You may be a nurse, but I'm neither sick nor disabled."

"Not physically, no." Victoria finished the apricot and dropped the pit back onto the tray. "Mikel's grandmother, Sonia, called me, you know. She's worried that Mikel won't, as she put it, 'come up to snuff.' From the way you dragged in alone last night, I'd guess he hasn't yet. How do you feel about him?"

Rachel had successfully avoided this subject until now. Somehow she didn't want to lie to her sister. "I love him," she admitted reluctantly. "But he…" Her voice trailed off.

"He's obtuse like a lot of men, right? Steve certainly was."

"He, well, he wants me." Rachel felt her face flush. She'd never talked this intimately to anyone.

"Of course. With no strings. Typical male. Not to worry—Zed and Karen have a barbecue planned."

Rachel blinked at her.

Victoria grinned. "Strange things have happened at this ranch when the whole gang gets together— you'll find out."

Deciding her sister wasn't going to explain, Rachel said, "Even if, well, if Mikel were to ask me to live with him, I don't know if I would. I mean, you said yourself Steve is gone a lot and it must be the same with Mikel. I don't know if I could keep moving from place to place. And yet I want to be with him." She sighed.

Moving the tray aside, Victoria reached out and hugged her. "It's not like that—I'm sorry if I gave you the wrong impression. Yes, I wish Steve were home more, but he does have our home to come to, which he does as much as he can."

She smiled. "As you saw for yourself, it really *is* home, complete with Heidi, Joker the dog and Bevins the cat. And me. Believe me, Steve knows how lucky he is. And so do I."

"I love your place in Virginia."

"So you and Mikel can buy a place near us and we can console each other when the guys are off on a bad guys hunt. We have a lot of catching up to do."

Which would be great, Rachel thought. Except Mikel had never mentioned love, much less marriage. If he'd been planning to ask her to live with him, as she suspected he might have been leading up to last night, surely he wouldn't be about to buy a house. Not that she needed more than an apartment, no, but she did need to feel it might be permanent. She wanted to belong somewhere.

She managed a smile for her sister. "Right now, I need to go back to the U.P. and start the courses for my master's degree."

Victoria raised her eyebrows. "You can take those anywhere."

"Yes, but I owe Aino and—"

"You know perfectly well Sonia is taking good care of him and that his granddaughter also lives with him. He doesn't need you."

Which was true.

Later, after showering and dressing in a new denim skirt and an off-the-shoulder cotton blouse she'd bought since she'd been in Nevada, Rachel wandered into the kitchen where she was quickly put to work fixing salad ingredients. It seemed the women did the inside work and the men the outside barbecuing.

By noon Rachel, her sister and Karen were joined by Karen's sisters-in-law, Jade and Linnea. Though she'd been confused at first, by now Rachel knew Jade was Zed and Talal's sister and that she was married to Dr. Nathan Walker. Tim was their adopted son. Linnea was married to Zed's twin Talal and their older daughter Yasmin was also adopted.

When Laura, Steve's sister, arrived, her husband, Shane, joined the men and they, along with the children, wandered off outside. Laura laid her baby daughter in one of the twin cradles in the living room and Linnea's older twin babies sat in high chairs in the kitchen where they could watch what was going on.

Everyone in this extended family of Victoria's was friendly and Rachel liked them all. At the same time, she didn't quite feel she was a part of them. When she finished her kitchen duty, she slipped into the living room to see Laura's baby. To her surprise, an older woman she hadn't yet met sat in a rocker with the baby in her lap.

"I'm Rachel Hill—that is, Reynaud," she said.

"The lost lamb who was found." The woman smiled warmly. "My name's Gert Severin and I belong to this crowd only by default."

The name clicked in her mind. This was Jade's doctor husband's colleague, a psychiatrist, if she remembered correctly.

Apparently her expression gave her away, because Gert said, "I see you've placed me. I'm really quite harmless."

Rachel smiled at the grandmotherly-looking woman, thinking it would be easy to relax and let down one's guard with Gert. Not that she needed the services of a psychiatrist. "Everyone here is so happy," she said, hearing the wistful tone in her voice with dismay.

"No one is happy all the time—that's a fallacy of the worst sort." Gert's voice was matter-of-fact and pleasant. "We think we should be and that just goes toward making us miserable."

"No one should be miserable all the time, either," Rachel found herself saying.

"True. Misery is a depressing companion. It behooves us to search for ways to rid ourselves of this darkness of the heart."

How? Rachel wanted to ask her, but caught herself before stepping over what well might be a professional boundary.

Gert offered her an encouraging smile. "If only we take the time and trouble to do it, many of us are well adjusted enough to look into both our minds and our hearts to find the path that best suits us at any given time."

General advice. Or was it? Troubled, she nodded at Gert, saying, "I'd best get back to work." Leaving the room, she paused and added, "Thank you."

Caught up once more in chores that had to be done, Rachel had no time to think of anything personal, especially when the women moved outside to join the men. Her gaze flew unerringly to Mikel, who was talking either to Zed or Talal. It was hard to tell them apart unless you heard them speak, since Talal had a slight foreign accent while Zed did not. To her surprise, Mikel was wearing blue jeans and a white T-shirt. No black?

As if conscious she was looking at him, he glanced her way, and for a moment, she felt they were somehow connected. But the moment passed and was gone.

"Rachel, would you help set up the croquet hoops?" Victoria asked. "The kids will want to play later and if they do the setup one or the other of them is always complaining it's wrong. We can get it done without interference now while they're in the pool."

"If you show me how."

"I've got a diagram." She handed over a folded paper.

The setup took time. Then a very noisy badminton game was organized, men against women. Rachel enjoyed herself, but she couldn't quite forget she really didn't belong to this fun-loving, close-knit family.

Aino and Eva are my family, she told herself. That's where I belong. They need me. She shook her head. That last wasn't true. Eva was a grown woman and Aino had found himself a wonderful companion in Sonia.

Reminded that she now had a mother and a sister, Rachel sighed. Her mother lived in a seniors community and her life was built around the activities there. Though she'd cried and thanked God her child had been found, Rachel knew her mother really didn't need her, except, of course, for visits.

Victoria had Steve and Heidi. Plus Joker and Bevins.

She noticed Mikel making his way toward her and her breath caught. Did she want to talk to him right now? The question didn't need to be answered because he got intercepted by Jade's husband, Nathan, and led away, presumably to do something with one of the barbecue grills.

Eventually, as the sun lowered, they ate. Everything was delicious, but Rachel didn't have much of an appetite. By the time they finished, the sun was easing behind the mountains. Then it was cleanup time—easy, because almost everything was disposable.

Jade got out her guitar and everyone sang along. In the midst of this, Heidi managed to grab the new dog and hugged him so hard that he yelped and nipped her. Though the skin wasn't broken, she wailed loudly and Victoria took her off to tend to the boo-boo.

"That kid of ours finds one disaster after another," Steve complained fondly. "She's been trying to get hold of that dog ever since we got here. Didn't listen to words of warning from either of us. Now maybe she'll leave him alone."

"Experience is the only teacher for some of us," Laura said, with a secret glance at her husband, who took her hand.

Since no one was paying any particular attention to her, Rachel decided this was a good time to slip away without being noticed. She really did need to be by herself. Deciding she wouldn't go anywhere near the gazebo, she wandered off toward the barn—red, like any respectable barn should be. Which made her realize how lucky she was to have been befriended by someone like Aino, who, no matter what, was always his own person, black barn and all.

She recalled how she'd once told Mikel he was like Aino, and he was in some ways—being his own person one of them.

The stable was next to the barn—an addition, actually, and she was about to go in and look at the horses when she heard someone whistling and turned.

"Looking for a cow to milk?" Mikel asked as he came up beside her.

"You followed me," she accused.

"What else? We haven't had a chance to exchange two words with each other today." He nodded at the barn. "Want to go in and see the kittens? Danny told me they don't have any tails."

"Manx?"

He shrugged. "I'm no cat expert."

Of course not. Pets meant strings. "Where are these kittens?" she asked, knowing exactly what he was going to say. When Aino had had a cat, she'd always chosen the loft for her litters.

"In the loft, Danny said." Mikel began whistling again.

"I've heard you whistle that tune before, but I don't recognize it," she said, stalling for time. Climbing into the loft with him would be agreeing to more than seeing Manx kittens, she knew. Should she?

"'Ochi Chorni.' It's a Russian folk song."

The words had a familiar sound. After a moment she realized why. "You whispered that in my ear when we were, well, in Aino's barn," she said.

"It translates as 'Dark Eyes'." He half smiled. "Which you once had."

Unsure how to take that—was he actually teasing her?—Rachel didn't reply.

"So, Tawny Eyes, care to climb into Zed's loft with me?" he asked.

She gazed at him, making up her mind. He wanted to make love with her, she knew. Despite everything, if she were honest, that's what she wanted, too, wasn't it?

Without giving him an answer, she sauntered toward the barn. A light over the door made it easy to see how to slide it open, but she deliberately waited for him to catch up and do the honors. Somehow it seemed appropriate.

Once he'd opened the door, he flicked on an interior light. In the connected stable, she heard a horse snuffle and shift its feet. The familiar barn smell gave her a sense of homecoming. The ladder to the loft was directly ahead. He gestured toward it.

Glancing at him, she said, "You first. I have a skirt on."

He grinned at her, as well he might, but she couldn't help—or explain—her attack of shyness.

As he climbed the ladder ahead of her, she stared at his blue-jeans-covered butt and asked, "What happened to the man in black?"

He reached the top and turned to look down at her. "Ever hear about the tiger who changed his stripes? That's me."

She raised her eyebrows.

He led her directly to the kittens and their mother, making her say, "Danny must have told you exactly where they were."

"He said mama cat kept hiding them in different places, but we special agents have our secret ways. Reconnaissance uncovered her latest nest in the hay."

"You mean you've already been up here?"

He shrugged.

Shaking her head, Rachel knelt and stretched a cautious hand toward the cat, who sniffed her fingers, showing no hostility, even when Rachel picked up an orange-and-white kitten with a tiny stub of a tail, snuggling it up against her cheek.

"Aren't they darling?" she cooed.

"If you say so."

"Oh, come on, there's nothing cuter than a kitten."

She held it out to him and he ran a cautious forefinger over its head. The kitten wailed, causing the mother cat to mew in protest. "Obviously I don't have the right touch where kittens are concerned," he said.

Rachel returned the kitten to its mother and rose from her knees. He took her hand and led her to where a blanket stretched across the hay. "Reconnaissance?" she asked, nodding toward the blanket.

"Okay, so I planned ahead," he muttered. "You can't deny hay prickles when you sit on it. We had to talk somewhere in private. Beside, I seem to recall telling you I'd bring a blanket next time. Which this is."

"Yes, but for all you know, Danny and the other kids will be swarming up the ladder any moment."

"No," he said. "They won't. I guarantee it. Please sit down."

When she did as he asked, he breathed a sigh of relief. The barn light was attached to a wall lower than the loft, so that shadows concealed her expression, but he knew she must have doubts.

"You think I brought you up here just to make love to you," he said.

She fingered the blanket. "Something like that, yes."

He put an arm around her shoulders, pulling her closer to him, but controlled his urge to kiss her.

"I'm not saying that isn't in the back of my mind, but I meant what I said—we need to talk."

"Why are you so sure the kids won't come into the barn?"

"Nathan."

"Dr. Walker? What does he have to do with anything?"

Mikel decided this was no time to reveal what Nathan had said to him in private, though the words still reverberated in his mind. "You want to find the entire gang circling you and Rachel?" Nathan had asked him. "Because that's what'll happen if you don't settle whatever you two have going for you. I know, because that's what they did to Jade and me, and I sure wouldn't want to repeat that confrontation. Believe me, it's embarrassing."

Then Nathan had gone into specifics. "If you love her, tell her so. If you want to be with her in whatever arrangement, get her to agree before you're forced to do it in public."

Mikel had stared at Nathan, hardly believing his ears. "But I'm not family, I'm a stranger."

Nathan chuckled. "You're family enough because you're Steve's buddy, so you've been accepted. And Rachel is his wife's sister. Think about it, man."

Mikel then button-holed Steve and got the same story. "The only reason Victoria and I escaped was because I beat them to it," Steve told him. "If I were you I'd take Doc's advice. And, by the way,

Victoria reports that Rachel is in love with you, if that makes any difference.''

To say he was rocked back on his heels was an understatement. Yet his surprise was as much from how he realized he felt about Rachel as from what Nathan and Steve had told him. He knew he and Rachel had to talk, and the sooner the better, so he got Nathan to keep the kids away from the barn. For some reason he'd known in his heart that she'd be drawn there.

In his heart. Where truth lay, according to Grandma Sonia.

''You haven't answered my question,'' Rachel said, bringing him back to the moment.

''About Nathan? I asked him to keep the kids away because we had some decisions to make.''

''We do?''

He nodded. ''And we're in this hayloft because it was in that U.P. hayloft where I first realized you were the one. The only one. It took me a while to accept this since I'm not too swift at looking into my heart. I love you, Rachel.'' He found the words to say far easier than he'd expected. Maybe because they *were* the truth.

''You—you do?''

''I've succumbed to a superior force.''

Snuggling closer, she laid her head on his shoulder and breathed his name, murmuring, ''I love you, too.''

He smiled to himself. "So I figure marriage is the only solution."

She jerked her head away. *"Marriage!"*

"Yeah—you must have heard of it since it's a venerable institution." His words were cooler than his emotions. Would she agree?

"I—you took me by surprise." Turning toward him, she folded herself into his arms.

"Before I kiss you, I need an answer."

"You mean you won't make love with me if I don't give you one?"

Damned if she wasn't teasing him. He gave a whoop of laughter. "Just try me."

"After due consideration," she said, "the answer is yes. Can we live in Virginia, where Victoria and Steve are?"

"Talk about planning ahead! But, hell, why not? End of conversation." He lowered his head and kissed her, and as always, the world faded into the distance. With all his heart he believed it would always be this way with the two of them. His last coherent thought was that his grandmother was right, as usual. Rachel was the only woman for him. She always would be.

Epilogue

"There's Mommy's car," Rachel told Heidi, who was sitting on the floor. Victoria sometimes dropped the little girl off at Rachel's when she wanted to run an errand, since the house she and Mikel had bought was conveniently near Steve and Victoria's. "We'd better get your jacket."

Heidi looked up from putting together the large plastic Lego pieces Rachel kept here for her to play with. "No," she said.

"Yes. Mommy will stay until you finish your creation, and then she'll take you home."

"Not crashun. Kitty."

"Okay, your kitty."

"You don't got kitty."

"No, we don't have any pets," Rachel told her.

Heidi gazed at her with her big blue eyes, enough to melt the hardest heart. "Poor Aunty."

Rachel felt anything but poor. Marriage to Mikel was even better than her dreams and it was wonderful living so close to her sister. Plus she'd been able to do some substitute teaching on occasion.

"Finish the kitty and we'll save him," she told Heidi, "but we have to put all the other pieces back in the box for next time."

The door opened enough for Victoria's head to poke through. "Okay to come in?"

"Mommy, look." Heidi brandished her creation.

Victoria entered. "That's a wonderful—" she paused, obviously searching for a resemblance to something.

"—kitty," Rachel finished.

"Oh, yes, it does look like Bevins," Victoria said.

"Not Bevins," Heidi insisted. "Aunty's kitty."

A few minutes later, with Rachel holding "her" kitty, Victoria persuaded Heidi into her jacket. As she bore her daughter off, Victoria grinned at Rachel and said, "So now you that you have a taste of what's in your not-so-far-away future, what do you think?"

"I can't wait," Rachel said.

Victoria rolled her eyes.

After they left, Rachel finished picking up the unused plastic pieces and set the box into the play cupboard that held toys for Heidi. Her niece could be a handful, but she was such a darling. She glanced at her watch, murmured "Oh-oh," and headed for the kitchen to check the stew in the Crock-Pot. Mikel would be home any time now and she wanted to make sure all the dinner fixings were close to ready.

When she heard his car pull into the garage, it was nearly an hour later than he'd told her, making her glad she'd planned on stew, a dish that only tasted better the longer it sat.

He came in through the back door and she started to reach up for a kiss, pausing when she realized he was carrying a grocery bag in one hand and, with his other, cradling something wrapped in his jacket.

"What've you got there?" she asked.

As she spoke, a tiny head poked out of the jacket and she stared into a kitten's golden eyes.

"Good heavens! That's a cat."

"I thought you liked them," he said, unwrapping it and exposing the scrawniest, dirtiest kitten she'd ever seen.

She reached for it. "Oh, Mikel, the poor little thing." The calico kitten clung to her, purring.

"Stopped to get gas. The guy running the place had just found the kitten in his Dumpster. Since it's too little to have crawled in, he figured someone had tossed it in there. He didn't want the cat, was going to call the animal shelter, so, well, I took Koshka."

"Koshka?"

"Russian for *cat*. The guy said it was a female and the name seemed to fit her."

If he'd named her, he really did mean to keep her. "I thought you weren't any too enthusiastic about cats."

He shrugged. "No one wanted this one. Besides, she's got eyes the color of yours."

Rachel reached up and gave him a quick kiss. "I knew there was a reason I married you," she said.

Later, after supper and after she'd given Koshka a bath and the kitten had eaten some of the cat food Mikel had brought home, she looked much more appealing. Holding her, Rachel sat on the couch with Mikel, then Koshka promptly crawled off her lap and onto his, where she curled up and closed her eyes.

"Hey," he protested, "who invited you?"

"She knows a rescuer when she sees one," Rachel told him, laughing, remembering how, at Aino's, he'd tried to discourage Metsa from following him around.

No strings, he told the dog.

He'd really surprised her by bringing home this kitten—two strings now, his wife and his kitten. Maybe it was time to tell him she had her own little surprise coming up in about seven months.

"Mikel," she said, snuggling closer, "how about it? Do you think you can adjust to a third string?"

He blinked, then his eyes widened. "Are you

telling me I get to be a father?'' Before she could answer he smiled at her, a happy grin that warmed her heart.

''Wife, cat, baby,'' he murmured as he reached for her. ''Love those entangling strings.''

* * * * *

SILHOUETTE®
SPECIAL EDITION™

AVAILABLE FROM 18TH JANUARY 2002

BACHELOR'S BABY PROMISE Barbara McMahon
That's My Baby!

Jared Montgomery would do anything rather than hold a fidgeting baby. Except now he was sharing his home with a newborn—and her lovely nanny, Jenny Stratford. How could he resist?

SEVEN MONTHS AND COUNTING... Myrna Temte
The Stockwells

When Rafe Stockwell discovered he'd fathered a child with Caroline Carlyle he proposed marriage—but Caroline rebuffed his proposal. So how will Rafe convince Caroline that he's never stopped loving her?

THE TIES THAT BIND Ginna Gray
A Family Bond

Outwardly Willa Simmons was infuriated by Zach Mahoney and would defy him at every turn. But when danger loomed, it was his powerful broad shoulders she turned to for protection.

UNEXPECTEDLY EXPECTING! Susan Mallery
Lone Star Canyon

Marriage-shy Nora Darby and Stephen Remington's public battle of the sexes had led to a night of private passion. Followed by an unexpected pregnancy...leaving them in a state of imminent parenthood and—shudder!—matrimony!

LOST-AND-FOUND GROOM Patricia McLinn
A Place Called Home

Three years after their son was conceived Daniel Delligatti is back to claim his child—and his wife. All Kendra has to do is learn to trust him again...

MONTANA MAIL-ORDER WIFE Charlotte Douglas
Identity Swap

Amnesia victim Rachel O'Riley didn't want a pretend marriage—she and Wade wanted to make it real. Then Wade uncovered a secret that changed everything...the woman in his arms *wasn't* Rachel O'Riley.